Trooper Dalton

After getting involved in a saloon-room brawl in Fort Lord, Dalton is arrested. His situation worsens when an unsympathetic judge sentences him to a year in jail unless he takes the alternative of signing up with the Plains Cavalry.

Dalton reckons that anything will be better than breaking rocks, but when he joins Company H – known as Company Hell – he soon regrets his decision. The troopers are a motley collection of prisoners recruited from jailhouses, or gunslingers running from arrest warrants.

As his fellow troopers are more determined to destroy the peace than to keep it, Dalton will need all his survival skills to serve out his term and all his ingenuity to defeat their plans.

Trooper Dalton

Ed Law

A Black Horse Western

ROBERT HALE · LONDON

© Ed Law 2012
First published in Great Britain 2012

ISBN 978-0-7090-9902-4

Robert Hale Limited
Clerkenwell House
Clerkenwell Green
London EC1R 0HT

www.halebooks.com

Typeset by
Derek Doyle & Associates, Shaw Heath
Printed and bound in Great Britain by
CPI Antony Rowe, Chippenham and Eastbourne

CHAPTER 1

'Arnold King's breaking everyone out!'

'Good,' Dalton said. He stretched out on his cot and then opened an eye to find that his eager cell-mate Tolbert North was beaming at him. 'When you've all gone, I can sleep in peace.'

Dalton placed a hand over his brow to shield his eyes from the bright morning sunlight, which was streaming in through the barred window above his head. The reduction in the light level didn't improve his mood.

His stomach was churning and the insistent throbbing in his head confirmed that last night he should have stopped drinking liquor after he'd emptied the first whiskey bottle.

It would have also helped his mood if he'd left the saloon before the fight broke out and if he hadn't thumped the deputy sheriff who had then tried to break up the fight.

'You not going, then?' Tolbert said.

'I've not come up before the judge yet. But I didn't do much wrong. I'll be out of here before my hangover clears up.'

Tolbert laughed as he matched Dalton's posture by lying back on his cot.

'You sure were roaring drunk when they threw you in here last night with the rest of them. What were you celebrating?'

'Being alive,' Dalton murmured. He rolled on to his side to put his back to Tolbert.

He hoped this movement would discourage his cellmate from asking him to explain his cryptic comment, as he didn't reckon he could cope with talking about his circumstances while his head was pounding.

The last year had been a bad one.

This time last year he'd had a home, a wife, good friends. Then illness had taken his wife and his life had fallen apart. Now he had taken to the wandering life, with most of that wandering being between saloons.

He didn't know what town he was in or what the date was. But he hoped that the anniversary of his wife's death had passed during the period in which he'd been drinking himself senseless, as that was the day he had promised himself he'd sober up.

Lying in a jailhouse facing a charge of being drunk and disorderly reinforced the fact that he'd now reached the bottom and it was time to move on.

With that thought in mind he rolled over, planning to be friendlier with his cellmate, but Tolbert was looking in the opposite direction.

Dalton then remembered the comment that had woken him. Before he could ask Tolbert if he had been serious, consternation broke out at the opposite end of the row of cells.

In the fourth cell away from him the deputy sheriff Ralph Rutherford had been dealing with one of the prisoners who had been rounded up last night. Now he was backing away through the cell door with his hands thrust high. The prisoner, presumably Arnold King, followed him out, holding a knife to the deputy's neck.

In the cells between them the prisoners remained silent, although they shot glances at each other and sat bolt upright on their cots. As they awaited developments Arnold beckoned Rutherford to move on towards the door that led to the law office.

As Arnold passed the cells he acknowledged each prisoner. In return they murmured supportive comments, until he reached Tolbert and Dalton's cell.

'I reckon,' Tolbert said, 'that the deputy's the only man on duty.'

Arnold nodded and then peered through the small barred window with confidence. He turned back, smiling.

'You're right,' he said. 'Nobody's out there. So are you all with me?'

The prisoners whooped with delight, and in short order Arnold removed Rutherford's ring of keys and threw them into the nearest cell. While the cell door rattled as the prisoners tried keys, Dalton lay back down on his cot and rubbed his forehead.

He only removed the hand when the first door opened and Tolbert got his turn with the keys.

'Last chance, Dalton,' Tolbert said as he picked a key to try. Dalton said nothing, so Tolbert continued: 'You'll regret staying here.'

'I'm staying,' Dalton said. 'But the best of luck.'

'I've already had plenty of luck today,' Tolbert said as the door opened. 'I just need a fast horse now.'

Dalton gave an appreciative smile. Then Tolbert passed the keys on and slipped out through the door to join Arnold and the other freed prisoners.

Within two minutes the other occupied cells had been opened, leaving Dalton as the only remaining prisoner.

'What's wrong with him?' Arnold muttered.

Dalton groaned, but thankfully Tolbert provided an answer.

'He's got a sore head,' he said.

The other prisoners laughed. Then they turned their attentions to completing their escape. While lying on his cot with his eyes closed, Dalton listened to their progress.

The door to the main office opened. Then the prisoners swarmed out into the office.

For the next few minutes wooden doors cracked and other furniture was toppled as the prisoners ransacked the office, presumably as they searched for firearms and anything else they could take.

Then silence descended, broken only with a few whispered comments. Dalton presumed they were now ready to burst outside and make a run for it.

As this was when their escape attempt could go wrong, he proved he hadn't been involved by closing the door to his cell. Then he curled up on his cot, where he waited to be discovered.

'Do it!'

The loud cry echoed in the office. Then a grunt of pain sounded.

Dalton drew his shoulders up to his ears trying to cut off the noises, but he failed when the thud of fist on flesh sounded, followed by another grunt and scuffling sounds. Dalton presumed that the escape attempt was going badly.

When two more thumps sounded, accompanied by a demand to keep quiet, he accepted it was going well and the deputy was taking a beating.

Dalton couldn't see into the law office, so he sat up. His head complained and his stomach lurched, but as he felt guilty about having hit Deputy Rutherford last night, with a shuffling gait he headed out of his cell and to the door.

With his back resting against the jamb, he considered the scene in the office. It was largely as he'd expected.

Arnold was enjoying himself exacting retribution on the hapless deputy. Two men were holding him up while Arnold delivered steady blows to his face that cracked his head back repeatedly.

Strangely, he'd been wrong about one aspect of the escape. When the prisoners had ransacked the office they hadn't armed themselves. Instead, they were watching the beating pensively, with their gazes occasionally straying to the main door.

'That's enough,' Dalton said.

Arnold delivered a punch to Rutherford's belly and then swung round to face Dalton.

'Am I making too much noise,' Arnold said, 'for that sore head of yours?'

'You sure are. I want to sleep, so I'd be obliged if you'd stop wasting your time in here and leave.'

Most of the prisoners smiled, but Arnold kept his expression stern and shook his head.

'I don't take orders from you.'

'You don't,' Dalton said. He pointed at the window. 'Nobody's out there, but soon someone will come and they'll order you around. After what you've done here they'll do it for a long time.'

Most of the prisoners nodded. Then they moved for the door including the men who had been holding Rutherford up. As the deputy dropped to the floor, Arnold glared at the prisoners.

'You're not leaving until I say you can go,' he said

with quiet menace.

Eight men swung round to face him, all shaking their heads in bemusement, but after Arnold had glared at them for several seconds, they straightened their backs in a surprising show of accepting his decision.

'But the town's waking up,' Tolbert said, peering out of the window. 'We have to get away.'

'You're not one of us,' Arnold said. 'I haven't decided yet if you're coming with us.'

Tolbert conceded his point with a shrug.

'I understand,' he murmured, as some of his truculence faded away. 'I'm obliged for this chance.'

Arnold shrugged his sleeve, bringing to hand the knife he'd used to effect his escape.

'Prove it. Stick the deputy.'

Arnold flipped the knife over and caught it by the blade. Then he held it out.

'I'm not doing that,' Tolbert said, aghast.

He cast worried glances at the other prisoners, seeking support, but he encountered only cold gazes. He ended his look around the room facing the more sympathetic Dalton.

Even though Dalton had spent only a night in Tolbert's company, and most of that time he'd been comatose, he stepped forward.

'Tolbert doesn't have to prove nothing,' he said. He held out a hand. 'I'll stick the deputy.'

Tolbert's mouth dropped open before he got over

his shock and sneered, but Arnold smiled. He swung the knife round to present it to Dalton, who moved on to take it.

He hefted the knife in his hand while looking down at Deputy Rutherford, who was still conscious enough to be aware of what was happening. The deputy looked up at him with scared eyes and Dalton gave him an appropriately surly glare. Then he gestured at Arnold to leave.

'I'm not going nowhere,' Arnold said, 'until Rutherford gets what he deserves.'

Dalton shrugged. Then, while swinging the knife from side to side, he moved in purposefully, making the deputy shuffle away on his back to avoid the blade. But Dalton didn't intend to carry out his threat. When the knife reached the end of its trajectory, he converted his forward motion into a sideways scramble.

A moment later the blade was thrust up against Arnold's neck, he had swung Arnold around, and he'd wrapped an arm around his shoulders.

'Now listen, Arnold,' Dalton muttered into his ear. 'I've got the worst hangover I've ever had and it's not making me sociable. I want to sleep, so run along while you still can.'

Every prisoner, aside from Arnold, considered the sudden change of circumstance with knowing nods.

Arnold stiffened his shoulders, seeming for a moment as if he'd test Dalton's resolve, but then he relaxed and gestured to the door.

With a relieved sigh, one man opened the door and peered outside. Then, after considering the scene, he beckoned the others to follow him out.

When the prisoner had slipped from view, Dalton released his tight grip from Arnold's shoulders and moved backwards.

The moment the blade left Arnold's neck, Arnold jerked his elbow backwards, aiming to jab it into Dalton's stomach, but Dalton had anticipated his move and he avoided the blow easily with a quick sidestep. Then he rocked forward and shoved Arnold on towards the door.

After three paces Arnold stopped his forward motion and swung round to face Dalton. The two men locked gazes until Arnold uttered a snort.

'Later, Dalton,' he said.

Then he turned on his heel and joined the other prisoners who had slipped outside. Tolbert was the last to leave and he stopped in the doorway to consider Dalton.

'You took a big risk there,' he said. 'You must want the alternative real bad.'

'My crime was minor,' Dalton said, tossing the knife on to the nearest desk.

'Then you'll suffer more than most.'

Dalton started to ask what he meant, but Tolbert glanced outside with an ear cocked. Then, with a last nod to Dalton, he hurried away leaving Dalton with the deputy.

Dalton knelt down beside Rutherford, who had now closed his eyes and was breathing deeply. His face was bruised and bloodied, but Dalton reckoned he'd come out of his ordeal without serious injury. So he left him where he lay and turned to go back to his cell.

'Stop right there,' a strident voice demanded behind him.

Dalton swirled round to find that Sheriff Cleland had arrived. The lawman had already turned a gun on him when outside the sounds of a commotion started up.

'I was going back to my cell,' Dalton said, pointing. 'I checked on the deputy. He'll be fine, but he'd still welcome some help.'

'I sure would,' Rutherford said from the floor, his voice grating after his ordeal. 'But knowing you didn't escape is making me feel better already.'

'I wasn't trying to escape,' Dalton spluttered, glaring down at him. 'If it hadn't been for me, Arnold King would have had you killed.'

Rutherford raised himself to a sitting position.

'That's right,' he said with a smirk. 'And from what I remember, you were the one holding the knife.'

CHAPTER 2

'One whole stinking year in jail for nothing,' Dalton grumbled when he returned to his cell after his trip to the courthouse.

'You were lucky,' Sheriff Cleland said as he opened his cell door. 'For trying to kill a lawman, I'd have given you twenty whole stinking years.'

Dalton opened his mouth to continue complaining, but then he chose discretion and returned to the cot he now wished he'd never left. When he saw that he wouldn't be alone in the jailhouse, he couldn't help but snort a rueful laugh.

Tolbert North was in the next cell, he being the only other prisoner here. He was sporting a livid bruise on his cheek along with an aggrieved scowl.

'Not go well, then?' Dalton asked when the sheriff had left them alone.

'I was too slow,' Tolbert muttered. 'Everyone else disappeared within minutes, but the law caught up with me.'

Dalton sighed. 'Seems we've both got a reason to regret helping Deputy Rutherford.'

Tolbert grunted that he agreed. Then he reverted to silence as he awaited his trip to court. He didn't have to wait for long, and when he returned Dalton didn't have to wait for long before hearing the surprising news.

'I chose the alternative,' Tolbert said, using a flat tone. While the sheriff held the cell door open, he collected his hat and jacket from where he'd left them on his cot. 'I didn't want to do it, but the judge didn't give me no choice.'

'You're leaving?' Dalton asked, sitting up on his cot.

Tolbert plodded on to the door, where he stopped. With his head lowered he delivered a long sigh.

'Sure. I couldn't face three years of breaking rocks.'

He started to explain, but Sheriff Cleland spoke up.

'Are you now saying you're interested too, Dalton?' he said with an irritated tone. 'Because this is your final chance.'

'I never got given a choice.'

'You did, but you were too busy grumbling about your head to hear it.' Cleland jerked his thumb over his shoulder indicating the law office. 'Come and sign up. Then I can enjoy a quiet jailhouse.'

16

Dalton didn't question his luck and, after being let out of his cell, he joined Tolbert when he presented himself before the provider of their salvation, who turned out to be an army officer.

Major Garrison stood in the office with a straight back, looking resplendent and shining in his blue uniform.

'So you don't want to waste away your lives in jail,' he announced, using an authoritative voice that made Tolbert stop slouching. It even made Dalton and the sheriff stand straighter.

'I don't,' Tolbert said with a gulp, 'and neither does he, Major Garrison.'

Garrison appraised Dalton and, from the narrowing of the eyes, he clearly found him inadequate.

'I've turned plenty of saloon room brawlers into disciplined fighting men. By the time you leave my care, if ever, I'll have you reading, writing and fit to hold your head up in anyone's company.'

'I can already read and write,' Dalton said.

'Then you're already one step ahead of the other enlisted men. You could go far.'

'And if I join up, how far do I have to go?' Dalton asked, having decided that even though he didn't want to join the Plains Cavalry, he hated the thought of spending a year in the jailhouse even more.

Garrison acknowledged his small joke with a thin smile.

'Only to the fort.' When Dalton furrowed his brow,

17

Garrison stepped back for a pace in surprise. 'You have noticed Fort Lord's most obvious feature, haven't you?'

Dalton didn't want to disappoint Garrison by admitting that when he'd ridden into town last night he'd been too drunk to notice anything other than the saloon sign.

So he gestured for Garrison to lead the way, which the major did with a glare that said that was the last time Dalton would give him an order.

At the door, Dalton glanced at the sheriff, who had already dismissed them from his thoughts. He had settled down on his chair with his hands behind his head and his feet resting on his desk.

Dalton couldn't help but notice that his chest was heaving with silent laughter.

Major Garrison had been right. Nobody should have failed to notice the fort.

The huge establishment stood on the edge of town, or to be more precise the town had sprung up around the stockade. Currently, only a small contingent of personnel was on duty, consisting of the guards at the gate along with a few others whom Dalton glimpsed amidst the buildings within the stockade.

Everyone carried out their duties efficiently and they gave Garrison the respect he demanded. So, by the time he led Dalton and Tolbert to the quartermaster storehouse, they were marching along.

They were issued with uniforms that almost fitted and which, they were promised, had been worn only once before. The threadbare nature of the clothes made Dalton doubt this was true and, more worryingly, Tolbert's uniform had a small, singed hole in the centre of the back that hadn't been stitched well.

Then they were led outside, sworn in, and taken away to complete the first vital task of their new life.

'See those horses?' Garrison announced when they reached the stables.

'Sure,' Tolbert said. He thought for a moment. 'Sure, *sir.*'

'See those shovels?'

'Sure, sir,' Tolbert and Dalton said together.

'You two are clearly observant and resourceful men. I'll leave you to figure out the rest.'

After saluting, Garrison left them to begin work caring for the twenty-five horses currently in the stables. There were four times as many empty stalls, so Dalton reckoned he could now see how he'd be spending the next year.

'You pleased you chose this?' Tolbert asked, as he picked up a shovel.

'It's better than counting bugs climbing up the wall,' Dalton said, joining him, 'and we're getting paid thirteen dollars a month.'

'I guess we are.'

Tolbert hadn't sounded pleased about the prospect, so, as he shovelled, Dalton asked his former cellmate the question that had been on his mind for the last few hours.

'Why were you in jail?' When Tolbert didn't reply, he continued. 'You were the only prisoner who hadn't been in that fight last night.'

Tolbert broke off from shovelling to consider him with his lips pursed until, with a sigh, he appeared to decide that he should tell him the truth.

'I shot my brother.' Tolbert raised his eyebrows and waited for Dalton's reaction. Dalton was silent as he struggled to find an appropriate reply, so Tolbert continued: 'I regret it and he's fine, but I shot him up.'

'Why?'

Tolbert rocked his head from side to side and then shrugged.

'He didn't shovel fast enough.'

Dalton laughed as he resumed working.

'Is there any chance he'll forgive you?'

'Sure. Mitchell forgives everyone. And that was the problem.' Tolbert gestured down the row of stalls. 'Maybe three years in here will make me feel I deserve that forgiveness.'

'It's got a better chance of working than if you'd escaped.'

Tolbert nodded slowly, suggesting he hadn't considered it that way before.

'This morning I panicked,' he said with a resigned air. 'But now I'll take the punishment I deserve.'

Then he started work again, his firm swings of the arms convincing Dalton that he didn't want to talk about his brother any more. But as they'd be spending plenty of time together, he was content to let Tolbert explain in his own time, if he chose to.

Later in the afternoon they got an even clearer idea of how their term of duty would pass when, having cleaned out the stables, Company H returned.

For the rest of the afternoon, their duties expanded to include shovel duties for all the horses while, after stable call, the returned troopers embarked on brushing and watering their steeds, polishing buttons and boots, and other menial tasks.

Clearly a trooper's life was a dull one, and that was fine with Dalton. It felt even finer when the supper call came and he and Tolbert got time to socialize.

The troop proved to be a rowdy bunch of men who displayed none of the military discipline Garrison had promised.

While they sat at the long benches in the mess hall and wolfed down their salted pork, hard bread, beans and rice, several men hailed Dalton and used his name, their familiarity making it appear that they'd met him before.

They were clearing away their plates when Dalton worked out that he'd met them in the saloon last night. Back then they hadn't worn their uniforms and they hadn't mentioned they were troopers.

Even stranger, they had started the fight that had culminated in his trip to the jailhouse.

He got a second shock when they left the mess hall and everyone headed to the barracks. He and Tolbert followed two men who had been prisoners in the jailhouse before they'd escaped. He bade Tolbert to draw back.

'You recognize them?' he asked.

'Sure,' Tolbert murmured. 'Perhaps that explains why they were eager to escape and how they went to ground quickly.'

'I can't believe nobody has disciplined them.'

As they approached their designated building Tolbert nodded unhappily. They would be the last ones to enter.

'I know, and worse, I thought the prisoners were violent outlaws with good reasons to run from the law.'

When they reached the door both men slipped in, to find that they were the subjects of their new associates' interest.

The troopers were either sitting up on their bed sacks or standing, and they were all facing Dalton and Tolbert, sporting eager grins that suggested they had planned mischief for the newcomers.

Behind them the door was slammed shut and two men moved in to stand before it. So, with no choice, the new recruits walked on between the bunks, their boots clattering in the quiet room.

As they passed they nodded to the troopers. In return they received amused smiles, until they reached the far end, where a group had gathered.

With a series of nudges and murmured comments, these men spread out to reveal the man they'd been surrounding: Arnold King. Now, like the others, he wore a uniform. His stripes showed that he was a sergeant, and therefore he was in charge of these troopers.

'Didn't reckon I'd see you again so soon, *Trooper* Dalton,' Arnold said, smirking.

'It's the same for me, *Sergeant* King,' Dalton said. 'The last time I saw you, you was escaping from the jailhouse.'

'You should have escaped with us. Then you might not have ended up in here.'

Dalton folded his arms. 'What's going on here? In this town, prisoners become troopers and troopers become prisoners. It don't make no sense.'

'It does. The thing is, no man enlists in the cavalry of his own free will. The recruits want to go missing, and so a friendly judge and an obliging commanding officer let them stay one step ahead of an arrest warrant or jail. The result is what you see here.'

Arnold gestured around him at the other troopers, many of whom grunted supportive comments.

'And what's that?'

'Company H. For some the H stands for hell. For others it stands for . . . hopportunity.' Arnold paused

23

as an appreciative round of laughter sounded at what was clearly an oft-repeated joke. 'The only question new recruits have to answer is, which one do they want?'

Dalton shrugged, then spoke loudly to address everyone.

'What you men did in the past is no concern of ours. So we'll take the hopportunity to serve our time quietly.'

Arnold shook his head. This encouraged the men to spread out and form a half-circle in front of Dalton and Tolbert. Behind them men got off their bunks to block their passage back down the aisle.

'The trouble is, you two crossed me.' Arnold shrugged his arm. A knife that looked like the one he'd used during his escape attempt slipped down his sleeve and into his hand. 'So you get hell.'

CHAPTER 3

Dalton leapt backwards with his arms spread wide apart. His quick motion let the knife slice air before his exposed chest.

The force of his movement made him backstep into the semi-circle of watching troopers. Obligingly, they caught him and pushed him back into the centre, forcing Dalton to twist away from Arnold's outstretched knife hand.

Then he stood his ground as he looked for an opening. His gaze took in the ranks of the watching men. He saw no sign that anyone would intervene.

Two men were holding Tolbert securely from behind. He'd been told that after Arnold had dealt with Dalton, he'd be forced to fight next.

'How did you get your knife back, Sergeant King?' Dalton asked, speaking calmly.

'You lost the right to ask questions,' Arnold said, 'when you defied me.'

'If I'd let you stick the deputy, you'd never have got to return here.'

'You don't know nothing about this town or my squad.' Arnold moved in slowly. 'And you won't get to learn nothing either.'

Arnold darted forward for a long pace, making Dalton take a step away from him, but the move had been only a feint. Arnold rocked back on his heels and laughed. Then, while bending over, he tossed the knife from hand to hand in a casual manner.

Dalton moved two paces to the side, seeking to get further away from him.

'You reckon you've avoided repercussions after your escape from the jailhouse, but you won't be able to explain away killing two men on their first day in the fort.'

Arnold straightened up and turned on the spot while gesturing to encourage a response. Accordingly, several men muttered about the newest recruits' stupidity.

'It sounds as if everyone will back up my story,' Arnold said as he continued to turn. He didn't speak again until he faced Dalton. 'And besides, you won't be the first to fail this test.'

When the semi-circle of men stamped on the floor, registering their approval, Arnold acknowledged the man who was making the most noise.

As that movement put his back to him, Dalton made his move. He bounded forward while thrusting his arms up, planning to grab Arnold around the chest from behind and then drive him on across the semi-circle.

Dalton had managed two paces when Arnold picked up on the approaching danger. Leading with his knife hand, Arnold swung round to face him. Dalton saw the blade coming and ducked beneath it, but the movement unbalanced him and sent him to his knees.

He used his momentum to keep tumbling. He rolled over on a shoulder and fetched up on his back, where he received glancing kicks from the enthusiastic onlookers while Arnold moved round to stand over him.

Arnold licked his lips as he searched for the safest way to stab Dalton while he lay supine. He ended up with the knife in his right hand. When he held it aimed downwards in a bunched fist, Dalton saw his intent and feinted away, drawing Arnold forward. Then, when Arnold jerked downwards, Dalton rolled the other way.

The blade slammed down into the floor behind him with what would have been a killing blow, before Dalton rolled into Arnold's feet. He upended him and sent him tumbling over his back, after which Dalton gained his feet quickly, aiming to turn the tables on his assailant.

His chances of survival grew when he saw the knife stuck point down in the wooden floor and quivering while Arnold lay sprawled beside it. Dalton leapt for the knife.

He went scrambling over Arnold's legs. His fingertips were brushing the knife when Arnold got his wits about him and kicked up, levering Dalton away from the weapon.

Dalton planted a foot to the floor, staying his motion. Then he leapt at Arnold, aiming to pin him down.

Hope sprang up in his heart that he would prevail, but Arnold had already anticipated his move; he rolled aside, causing Dalton to land on his chest.

Dalton didn't mind that response as it took his opponent away from the knife. So when he and Arnold got to their feet, he stood crouched forward, as Arnold had done previously, guarding the knife until he could claim it.

'Time to see if you've got any fight in you,' Dalton said, 'now we're even.'

The two men feinted right and then left with their fists bunched as they sought an opening, until Arnold stood upright and smiled. With a casual gesture he held up a hand and a moment later, footfalls scrambled behind Dalton. Then the knife went winging over Dalton's shoulder.

'I have something better,' Arnold said, plucking the knife from the air. 'I'm among men who follow my orders. You're not.'

Dalton lowered his head in a show of defeat.

Fortunately, Arnold took the bait. He moved in quickly and directed a wild slash that aimed to slice the blade into Dalton's shoulder.

At the last moment Dalton dropped to his knees, letting the blade pass harmlessly over his back. Then he drove off from the floor.

He caught Arnold in the stomach with his shoulder, then pushed him on across the encircling men. He didn't dare continue this motion for long for fear of Arnold stabbing him in the back. After three paces he shoved the sergeant aside.

Arnold went sprawling to the floor on his back, but he kept a firm grip of the knife. Dalton, when he loomed over him, kept his distance.

'I've got something that's better than men who do what they're told,' Dalton said. 'I beat you back in the jailhouse. So I know I can do the same here.'

This insult made Arnold's face redden and, as Dalton had expected, he didn't wait to gather his breath. He scrambled to his feet, but his tumble had weakened him and he teetered to one side.

His unplanned motion moved him towards the two men who were holding Tolbert. Their prisoner added to his discomfort by sticking out a leg and tripping him up.

Arnold kept his balance but several onlookers snorted laughs, giving Dalton hope that the sergeant wouldn't keep his authority for long.

'You just lost your last chance to live,' Arnold

murmured, swinging round to face him.

'Kill me and you'll lose a valuable trooper,' Dalton said, speaking confidently. 'Even unarmed I can fight better than any man here. When armed, I'll defeat anyone who stands in our way.'

Dalton looked around him. He received a few nods, along with murmured appreciative comments. Better still, two men drifted away from the circle as Arnold's support eroded.

Arnold shook his head. 'This is no normal squad, Dalton. That boast means nothing here.'

This time Arnold took his time in moving in. He held his knife close to his chest while looking for an opening. The two men circled each other.

Arnold's delay in acting gave Dalton time to think; he wondered why his previous statement hadn't gathered more support than it had. A look at the motley collection of troopers, along with a recollection of the odd way he'd been recruited gave Dalton the answer.

He stopped circling, stood tall, and spread his hands.

'I'd gathered the rules are different here,' he said with his head held high. 'So you should be pleased I joined up to avoid a long stretch in jail. I can be useful to you.'

'You're a nobody,' Arnold said with a dismissive wave of the knife. 'You got thrown in jail after that fight.'

'I did, but I was lucky nobody checked up on what else I'd done.' Dalton nodded at Tolbert. 'Except even I wouldn't shoot up my own brother.'

One of Tolbert's captors released him to get a better look at him. Picking up on Dalton's ruse, Tolbert did his best to look mean with a snarl.

A few moments later several other men in the semi-circle broke away and made off to their bunks as their willingness to see the newcomers suffer faded. Arnold eyed them with irritation until, with a shake of the head, he dismissed the matter.

'You two may think you're tough,' he said, talking loudly to address them as well as the departing stragglers, 'but you're not tough enough to join my squad.'

'But we have no problem with you,' Dalton said, speaking quietly to try to reduce Arnold's animosity, 'other than you wanted to kill that deputy lawman. Now that matter's over with, we should be able to cope with each other for the next year.'

Arnold had been rocking back and forth on his toes as he prepared to charge towards him, but Dalton's last words made him chuckle. Then, when he liked the sound, he laughed louder and slapped his thigh.

'You believed Major Garrison when he said you'd be here for a year?' Arnold threw back his head and forced out another exuberant laugh.

'That's what he said.' Dalton looked at Tolbert for

support. Tolbert nodded.

'Yeah,' Tolbert said. 'I got three years in the cavalry instead of three years in jail. It'll be the same for—'

'You're fools.' Arnold looked from one man to the other, lengthening out the time before he explained. 'The minimum term is five years.'

Dalton winced, remembering how the major had been surprised he'd joined up to avoid a one-year sentence.

'We don't believe you,' he said without conviction.

'Believe what you will. It won't matter none because you won't serve out that time.' Arnold hurled the knife to the floor. As it sliced into the wood, point down between them, he snorted one last chuckle. 'I don't need to kill you tonight because tomorrow you're going on your first mission. It'll also be your last.'

CHAPTER 4

'Today, men,' Major Garrison said, his authoritative voice echoing in the square and making the assembled troopers stand up straight, 'you are to track north along Black Creek to Jackman City. I have received a report that yesterday a homestead was burnt down. Your presence and vigilance will reassure the townsfolk.'

With reveille, roll call and his brief orders delivered, he exchanged salutes with Sergeant Arnold King. Then the complement of twenty-five troopers was dismissed. With sunup still an hour away, Arnold led his squad out of the fort.

Last night Dalton and Tolbert had picked a spare bunk in the corner of the barracks. Then, to avoid antagonizing the troopers again, they hadn't engaged anyone in conversation and instead they had gone to sleep quickly, sleeping two to a bunk head to toe like everyone else. So this morning they still weren't sure if Arnold's taunt about the length of their term had been a valid one.

Both of them figured that they could check whether he'd told the truth later, but only if they survived Arnold's other taunt.

They were a mile out of the fort when Arnold drew aside and then let the troopers ride on by until he could fall in beside Dalton and Tolbert. They rode on for another mile, during which time he appraised them with an amused gleam in his eye before he spoke.

'When we reach Jackman City,' he said, 'I'm sending you two on a special mission.'

'Which is?' Dalton asked.

'That's no concern of yours yet.' Arnold smirked. 'You just follow orders, Trooper Dalton and Trooper North.'

Dalton straightened his back. 'We're here to serve, sir.'

With a lick of the lips, Arnold appeared to decide not to taunt them any more. He hurried his horse on.

'As he's sending us somewhere,' Tolbert said when Arnold had returned to the front, 'we must hope that last night he was only trying to worry us.'

Dalton shrugged. 'Or he meant that this special mission is the way he'll organize our deaths.'

The suggestion made Tolbert gulp, but he said nothing more. For the next few hours they settled into riding at a steady trot.

Later that morning when they halted for a break, the other troopers spoke to them in a normal manner, as if the fight last night hadn't happened. But that didn't improve their spirits for long when they learnt that Arnold's other taunt had been truthful.

The minimum term everyone had signed up for was five years.

When they resumed riding, Dalton and Tolbert didn't speak again other than to discuss what they thought the punishment would be for desertion. They both thought it would be a heavier price than serving out their five-year terms.

The sun was at its highest and they had yet to reach Jackman City when they veered away from the river. Then, without preamble, Arnold led them to the wrecked house.

The building presented a less devastated scene than Dalton had been led to expect. The house was largely intact. Only half of the roof shingles had been burnt and even those were only charred.

Some roof timbers had fallen into the house, but they were also rotten and coated in mildew. The house itself and surrounding area appeared neglected, as if it had been abandoned some time ago.

Arnold ordered two men to explore the building, which they did in a bored, casual manner, mooching around the outskirts and then kicking over fallen timbers. Arnold and the others milled around in an equally bored manner until a rider approached.

He turned out to be Charles Mayweather, a rancher who owned most of the land south of Jackman City. Even though the fire had taken place on his land, he appeared unconcerned and he gazed upon the mass of troopers with bewilderment.

'We folk were getting on fine without the army storming around scaring our cattle,' Charles said. 'So why has a small fire in a disused building worried you?'

'Its cause is unknown,' Arnold said sitting tall in the saddle. 'That's worrying.'

Charles shook his head and then pointed. 'My ranch hands saw the culprit riding away towards the river. They chased him off and it was clear he was just a lone troublemaker.'

Arnold looked where Charles was pointing.

'In that case I'd be obliged if you'd show us where this man went.' He waited for a response, but when Charles merely widened his eyes, Arnold put on an ingratiating smile and lowered his voice. 'The sooner you help us, the sooner we'll leave.'

Charles slapped a fist against his thigh.

'I'll show you around,' he muttered. 'Perhaps then you'll accept that this doesn't concern you and go and annoy someone else.'

'You're most gracious.' Arnold gestured to Dalton

and Tolbert to approach. 'Show these two men around while we examine the building.'

Charles cast an irritated glare at Dalton and Tolbert and then at the bulk of the troopers, who wouldn't be accompanying them. His angry glare showed that the obvious question was on his lips: why were only two men going with him? but he chose not to voice it. With a sharp tug of the reins, he moved on towards the river.

'Any instructions, sir?' Dalton asked Arnold when the rancher had moved out of earshot.

'Keep him busy and feeling useful for as long as you can, Trooper Dalton,' Arnold said using a surprisingly reasonable tone. 'He can stir up trouble if he isn't happy that we came out here to deal with what looks like a trivial matter.'

Dalton accepted his orders with a salute and, with Tolbert at his side, he rode on after Charles. When they were ten yards away, Arnold said something to the troopers who were staying behind that made them laugh, but Dalton didn't acknowledge that he'd heard.

Tolbert didn't show the same forbearance. He glanced over his shoulder and then drew closer, bidding Dalton to slow so they wouldn't catch up with Charles too quickly.

'You got any idea what's going on here?' he asked.

'No,' Dalton said, 'but I reckon that's normal for a trooper.'

'Perhaps, but Arnold had already decided to send us off with Charles before we even got here. And somebody should have said the fire wasn't serious enough to make it worth us coming out here.'

Dalton nodded and this time he looked back at the house where Arnold's men had now dismounted. They had gathered in a group to receive his instructions.

'Nothing about this mission or these troopers makes sense, but at least Arnold's not gone through with his threat to kill us yet. So I reckon we should carry out his orders and then get back to the fort safely.'

Tolbert agreed with this sentiment and they hurried on to join their new companion, who was as disgruntled as he had been earlier. But Charles said nothing until they reached the creek, where he pointed along the banks, indicating the quiet scene.

'He went upriver,' he said. 'I'm a busy man, so is that all you need to know?'

As Arnold had done earlier, Dalton smiled and maintained a friendly tone.

'We'd gathered you don't want our help, but don't be angry with us. We only joined up yesterday.'

Charles looked from one man to the other with contempt.

'So what are you two running from?'

'I punched Deputy Ralph Rutherford.' Dalton pointed at Tolbert. 'He shot up his brother.'

Charles considered this information and then took the opportunity to lighten his mood by flashing them quick smiles.

'Then you're saints compared to Arnold King and the rest of those men. Take my advice: stay out of their way and you might not come out of your term worse men than when you joined up.'

'We intend to.' Then, with Charles appearing as if he'd be more responsive, Dalton nodded back at the burnt house. 'Why are you sure that this lone fire starter was nothing to worry about?'

Charles firmed his jaw, making it appear as if he wouldn't reply but, after he'd looked upriver he shrugged, seemingly accepting that he should indulge the troopers. He rode on with them at a fast walking pace while he told them the story of the last few years.

When the Plains Cavalry had been stationed at Fort Lord ten years previously the area had desperately needed their help, but two years of fighting had driven the marauding Cherokees away. They hadn't returned and the fort had ended up patrolling further afield in search of trouble as they sought to maintain the homesteaders' confidence.

The need for the patrols became less and less, and these days the only fighting the troop carried out was of the kind that had got Dalton and the others thrown in jail.

This change in circumstance was breeding resentment amongst people who had once been delighted to have the troopers around.

'So,' Charles said, completing his explanation, 'satisfy yourself quickly and let me get back to work. I'm losing money every hour I spend entertaining you folk.'

Dalton offered a reassuring smile, but he had his orders. He and Tolbert dallied for as long as they dared without the risk of drawing suspicion on themselves.

Under the guise of being a newcomer to the area, Dalton questioned Charles about anything that crossed his mind. Later, when his questions started irritating the rancher, he and Tolbert dismounted at every significant landmark to consider the ground and search for tracks.

As expected, they found no sign of the man's passage or anything else of interest. So, when they came to a sweep of the river from where they could see across the plains for miles in all directions, Charles drew his horse to a halt. A mile away stood his ranch house, and when he turned to it Dalton couldn't think of a way to detain him for any longer.

'How do we get back to the burnt-out house?' he asked lamely.

Charles pointed downriver and then, without further comment, he moved on, leaving Dalton and Tolbert with no choice but to follow him and hope that a valid excuse to delay him would present itself.

Unfortunately, they got their chance sooner than

they expected when Charles halted and drew their attention to the ranch.

Dalton narrowed his eyes and saw that a commotion was taking place. They were still a half-mile away, so Dalton couldn't be sure what was happening, but blue-uniformed riders were milling around.

'What are they doing here?' Charles demanded, swirling round to face the pair.

'I don't know,' Dalton said, 'but I'd guess Sergeant King found something and he went there to look for you.'

'But he knows I'm with you. . . .' Charles winced and then waved at them angrily. 'You two asked your idiotic questions to keep me away from the ranch.'

He glared at them, but when neither man could find a reply he moved on towards his house, speeding quickly to a gallop.

Dalton and Tolbert looked at each other with worried expressions. Then they hurried on after Charles.

They were 200 yards from the ranch gates when they got the first inkling of what was happening; a gunshot tore out and that initiated a rapid exchange of fire.

The riders within the gates separated, the troopers hurrying away towards a barn that stood to the left of the gates while the other men, presumably ranch hands, ran for the ranch house.

Repeated gunfire rang out as some men scurried

into hiding while others paused in their attempts to flee to shoot at the invaders. By the time Charles reached the gates Dalton saw two ranch hands lying motionless on the ground.

Charles looked over his shoulder at them with a worried expression. Dalton raised a hand to show they weren't a threat. Charles scowled at them again before trailing around the fence, taking a route to the ranch house that avoided going close to the barn.

A few moments later Dalton and Tolbert arrived at the gates, where they stopped to assess the situation.

The burst of gunfire had now ceased, the troopers having found cover. Aside from a ranch hand, who covered Charles from the doorway of the house as he took a roundabout way towards it, nobody was visible.

'This situation didn't happen by accident,' Tolbert said.

Dalton nodded. 'I reckon Arnold's final taunt last night wasn't a threat, after all. He set us up to take the blame for this.'

'Then I'm pleased we're no good at following orders.'

Dalton pointed at the barn. 'Come on. Let's find out what Arnold's up to. Then we can fail to do what we're told to do some more.'

Tolbert grunted that he agreed and they headed off in the opposite direction to the one Charles had taken.

By now, Charles was dismounting outside the

ranch house. When he moved to hurry along the porch, two of Arnold's troopers emerged from a side door in the barn to take shots at him.

Their efforts attracted retaliatory gunfire from the ranch house. Splinters sprayed from the barn wall and glass shattered in a ranch window as the two groups traded volleys of lead before everyone hurried back into hiding.

When there'd been silence for a minute, Dalton and Tolbert used the break to dismount quickly and then run to the side doorway. They picked a route that ensured that the troopers would see them and so were waved inside to face Arnold King.

When they'd gathered their breath Arnold considered them with a mixture of surprise and amusement gleaming in his eyes.

'I thought you'd be able to entertain Charles for longer than that, Trooper Dalton,' he said simply.

'If we'd known what you were planning, sir,' Dalton said, 'we'd have tried to delay him for longer.' He raised an eyebrow, requesting an explanation.

Before replying Arnold looked around the gathered troopers. The men, who were paying attention to their conversation, nodded. He beckoned the pair to walk with him to the wide doors at the front of the barn, from where they had a good view of the house.

'It's simple,' Arnold said. 'We're all recruited from jailhouses or we're outlaws avoiding arrest warrants. Major Garrison reckoned military discipline would make us change our ways, but we reckoned differ-ently. It just gave us more firepower.'

Dalton nodded. 'And why is Charles on the receiv-ing end of that firepower?'

'Charles is a rich man.' Arnold turned from con-sidering the terrain to face them. 'I intend to relieve him of that problem.'

Dalton took a pace to the side so that he wouldn't be visible from the ranch house.

'In that case,' he said, 'what do you want us to do?'

CHAPTER 5

'You realize Arnold's given us the most dangerous part of this mission,' Tolbert said, 'don't you?'

'I know,' Dalton replied. 'But at least it gives us a chance to stop him.'

Tolbert nodded and shuffled the coil of rope back over his shoulder. He turned away and continued snaking along the depression that led away from the back of the ranch house.

As long as they kept their heads down they couldn't be seen from the house. The barn had now disappeared from view behind them leaving them with just a limited view of the terrain ahead.

Dalton followed Tolbert. After the two of them had shuffled along for another thirty yards the depression flattened out, leaving them out on open land. They looked around for new cover, but they couldn't see any suitable positions close by, so they adopted crouched positions, ready to leap back into the depression if they were seen.

The back of the house had only a set of barred double doors and a single shuttered window, as Arnold had promised, so they ran on and pressed themselves to the wall.

Dalton counted to ten and then, as there had been no response, Tolbert dropped the rope on the ground and they split up to check along the length of the wall.

When they joined up again, they both confirmed that they couldn't see into, or be seen from, the house. So Dalton looked around the corner of the building to the barn, where Arnold was standing beyond the doorway in the shadows.

Dalton spread his hands and shook his head, conveying what they had found. Arnold replied with a series of short gestures that told them to complete their orders.

Dalton returned an assenting wave, then side-stepped along the wall to rejoin Tolbert.

'How much longer are we going to follow his orders?' Tolbert whispered, eyeing the rope at his feet.

'Until we're in a position to stop this raid,' Dalton said, picking up the rope reluctantly. 'Then we turn on him and help Charles.'

'Agreed,' Tolbert said. 'But Charles is likely to shoot us before we can explain ourselves.'

Dalton replied with a worried nod, but before they

could start planning how they would avoid that happening Arnold's assault on the house began in earnest.

Rapid shouted orders designed to instil fear broke out at the front of the house accompanied by even more rapid gunfire.

Dalton and Tolbert moved on to the door where, as they'd been instructed, they looped the rope around the heavy and locked-down bar. By the time they'd tightened the rope an open wagon, which the troopers had purloined from the barn, came rattling around the corner of the house. The driver swung the wagon round and turned its back to the wall.

Tolbert glanced at Dalton, silently asking him if this was the right moment for them to change sides, but the troopers on the wagon took that opportunity away from them.

The driver stopped the wagon while the other man leapt down and quickly looped the free end of the rope around a hook on the backboard. Then he beckoned the driver to move on while he leapt into the back.

The wagon moved forward, stretching the rope taut. For several seconds the door held and the horses strained until, with an explosion of wood, the door burst outwards. Then it was dragged along the ground until the driver turned in a small circle and drew alongside the doorway.

Only then did the two troopers turn to Tolbert and

Dalton and beckon them to head into the house first.

The pair moved on to the doorway. Dalton couldn't hear any noises coming from within, so he slipped inside, but then he turned to the right and stood against the wall.

When Tolbert followed him in, Dalton got his attention and pointed, telling him to stand by the wall on the opposite side of the door. Then Dalton listened to the sounds of the battle that was raging at the front of the house while he took stock of the situation.

He was in a large room in which several empty crates were lying around. A single door in the corner led, presumably, to the rest of the house.

'What's happening in there?' one of the troopers shouted from outside.

'We've found something interesting,' Dalton called. 'Come in and see what you think.'

He caught Tolbert's eye to coordinate their actions and he received a nod. A few moments later one man came in and peered around, his eyes narrowing as he looked around the darker interior.

When he moved on he walked past Dalton. He managed two paces before Dalton stepped up to him from behind and, with bunched fists, swung a double-handed blow at the back of his neck.

The trooper sensed the blow coming and flinched away, but Dalton's fists still caught his shoulder and swung him round. Dalton helped him on his way with a quick shove that threw him against the wall with which his forehead collided with a thud.

As Dalton grabbed the man's shoulder and drew him back ready to slam him against the wall for a second time, the other trooper came in and walked into Tolbert's swinging punch that sent him reeling outside.

Tolbert followed him out through the doorway while Dalton concentrated on subduing his opponent. He threw him face first at the wall, making the man groan as he rebounded. Then he dropped to his knees and on to his side.

Dalton rolled him over to find he was out cold. When he looked up Tolbert was dragging his opponent in through the door backwards, his heels kicking dust.

He deposited him next to the other man. Then he slapped his hands together while mouthing numbers quietly to himself.

'That's two down, twenty-one to go,' he declared.

Dalton patted his back while smiling at his optimistic outlook.

'It sure feels good to fight back,' he said, turning to the internal door.

'Yeah,' Tolbert said. 'Now we just have to convince Charles that we're not on Arnold's side.'

Dalton nodded and hurried on to the door where he heard only the sounds of the skirmish out at the front. It had now lessened in intensity, and only isolated gunshots were ringing out.

He edged the door open for a fraction, to be confronted with a wide corridor, so he leaned his head to the wall so as to see further.

He couldn't see anyone, although through the open door sounds of what was going on came to him more clearly. As he could hear talking, he could tell that the ranch hands must be close by.

With a hand thrust through the doorway, he tried to widen the gap, but the door rattled to a halt. When he looked down, he saw that, like the outside door, it had been heavily barred, except in this case the bar was on the other side.

Unlike the main door, there was no obvious way it could be opened. He beckoned Tolbert to offer suggestions, but Tolbert had stopped ten feet from the door.

Tolbert was facing the wall. He had raised a sheet that had been thrown over a collection of objects. With a preoccupied air, he kicked an empty crate aside and then tapped a foot against the next crate.

'Leave those where they are,' Dalton said. 'There's nothing interesting in here.'

Tolbert raised an eyebrow, then swung the sheet away to reveal what had interested him. Amidst the crates, a safe stood against the wall.

Dalton quietly closed the door and joined Tolbert. He helped him to move the rest of the crates aside, so giving the pair of them a clear view of the four-foot tall safe.

Experimentally, Dalton raised a corner, but he could move it only a few inches off the floor. He reckoned this meant the safe was robust enough to contain something interesting.

Then he tried the door. It was locked and it had a circular combination lock, adding credence to the possibility that something valuable was within.

The barred doors also suggested that this safe was what Arnold had come here to steal.

'If Arnold knows this was stored away in here,' Tolbert said, 'he'll come round to the back soon.'

Dalton stood back. 'Or perhaps he's engaging Charles at the front of the house to keep his attention there and make him believe he doesn't know about it.'

Tolbert considered, then nodded. 'It's too heavy to take into the house, even if we could get through the barred door. So how do we help Charles keep this out of his clutches?'

Dalton stood back and considered the almost empty room. The two troopers were still lying comatose and, through the wide doorway, he could see the open wagon they had brought, along with the rope and the attached door lying behind.

A wild idea tapped at his mind.

He shook it away, but it returned. Then it took root and developed branches that grabbed him and held him tightly.

When he looked at Tolbert his new friend stared at him with wide eyes, suggesting he'd had the same dangerous idea.

'Will it work?' Dalton whispered.

'It's utter madness,' Tolbert said. 'It's guaranteed to fail and it's sure to get us into a whole heap of trouble with Arnold's troopers, Charles Mayweather, Major Garrison, the law, in fact everyone, because nobody will believe we did it to help Charles.'

Dalton nodded. The two men stood in silence for several seconds considering each other.

'You get the wagon,' Dalton said. 'I'll attach the rope.'

Five minutes later they were ready to leave.

The two men sat on the wagon facing east and away from Black Creek. Behind them the safe lay on the door, both the door and safe being secured with rope to the back of the wagon.

'Where now?' Tolbert said.

Dalton pointed. 'That way.'

Tolbert raised the reins. 'I guess this means we're now deserters.'

'Only if we're still alive come sundown.'

Sundown found Dalton and Tolbert sitting under an overhang on the riverbank. The wagon and its cargo of door and safe stood beside them.

The wagon would be visible to anyone who came close, but this was the nearest suitable place to hole up that they'd noticed when they'd been scouting around with Charles earlier.

While they'd been riding away from the ranch the gun battle behind them had grown in intensity, though as they rode on the rattle of gunshots had receded into the distance. Luckily, nobody had followed them over the circuitous route they'd taken to get here.

Three hours later they had yet to see any sign of pursuit, so they were hopeful that they could remain free at least until dark.

What they would do then they hadn't yet decided. Neither were they sure that their gamble had been justified.

Accordingly, Tolbert joined Dalton in considering the safe. They took it in turns to spin the wheel of the combination lock in an idle manner, hoping they would fortuitously happen across the correct combination.

The safe remained resolutely closed, so the heavy thuds that had sounded within when they'd first moved it remained the extent of their knowledge about its contents.

'We moving on when it gets dark?' Tolbert asked.

'Yeah,' Dalton said. 'I reckon we should put some distance between Arnold and us. But if he's closing in on us I don't reckon we can outrun him all the way back to the fort with that heavy safe in tow.'

'Yeah,' Tolbert murmured in a distracted way.

'We'd have a better chance if we could stash it away somewhere until we can alert Major Garrison about what Arnold tried to do.'

'Agreed, but I don't know the area well enough to suggest where.'

Dalton looked at Tolbert for ideas, but Tolbert frowned and wandered away to look downriver. Then he climbed the bank to look back towards the ranch house.

His pensive expression showed where he was thinking about taking them, but Dalton waited for him to offer it.

'There is one place,' Tolbert said at last. He clambered back down the bank and gave a thin smile.

Dalton returned the smile. 'Then let's hope your brother Mitchell doesn't shoot you up when you return home.'

CHAPTER 6

'Mitchell would never shoot me,' Tolbert said after they'd ridden along through the dark for a while.

'Then no matter what the problem is between you and him,' Dalton said, 'he sounds like a good brother.'

'He sure is, and that's the problem.'

Tolbert rode on and, as this was the second time he'd said something cryptic along these lines, Dalton reckoned he was close to talking about the situation between them.

'The important thing is that he'll hide us,' Dalton prompted.

'He will, but he won't hide the safe.' Tolbert considered his partner, with the upper half of his face in shadows and his mouth in moonlight. He gnawed his lip. 'His chapel at Rocky Point isn't big enough.'

'Ah,' Dalton said, now getting an inkling of the issues they might have argued about. 'So, in your eyes, he's the decent brother who always does the right thing, is he?'

'Yeah, and I'm the brother who always does the wrong thing.' Tolbert sighed and, having revealed his shame, he relaxed. With an easier air, he continued: 'I have no problem with having a priest for a brother and he has no problem with having someone like me for a brother. So I reckon we'd get on fine if he wasn't determined to waste away his life on his ridiculous plan for the chapel.'

'And what is that plan?' Dalton asked after Tolbert had been silent for a while.

Tolbert frowned. 'It'll be best to let you see for yourself. Then you might understand why he annoys me so much.'

He said nothing else on the subject that night. The pair of them rode along as steadily and as unobtrusively as possible. They neither saw nor heard any signs of pursuit, so, while the moonlight held, they covered over half the distance to Rocky Point.

When full darkness arrived, they slept lying beneath the sheet that had covered the safe. At first light the cold woke both men from their fitful slumbers and so they moved on.

It was mid-morning when they approached their destination.

Dalton judged that Rocky Point stood at one corner of a triangle with equal-length sides that took in Jackman City and Fort Lord.

The community had spread out around the chapel, while the feature that had given the settlement its name was a rocky monolith. It was around 400 feet high and it stood out on the plains like a plump soldier standing to attention.

This natural feature towered above the settlement of around twenty buildings, all of which were crudely constructed, the stone-built chapel being the most robust.

However, when they were closer to the chapel Tolbert took a circuitous route that let Dalton see the building from the other side showing him that his first impression had been wrong.

One long wall of the chapel was solid, but that was the only complete side. There was no roof and the other three sides had been largely demolished. The stone blocks had been laid out on the ground over a wide area.

'It's a pity the building fell down,' Dalton said. 'I'd guess your brother has made it his mission to rebuild it.'

'Oh yes,' Tolbert murmured. His tone was distracted because a priest, presumably Mitchell, had emerged from behind the chapel to await their arrival.

Tolbert drew up fifty yards away from the building, this being a position where their trailing cargo wouldn't be obvious immediately. Dalton stayed on the seat and let Tolbert jump down alone and walk on for a few paces. Then he waited for Mitchell to come to him.

Mitchell's right arm was in a sling, but he was smiling.

'I'm pleased you've returned,' he said. 'And I forgive you.'

Tolbert cast Dalton a quick look that said he'd told him this would happen and then moved on to face his brother.

'And I'm pleased you're not seriously hurt.' He spread his arms, drawing Mitchell's attention to his uniform. 'Either way, I've made a big change in my life.'

Mitchell nodded approvingly. 'We both have a calling to follow now. Yours may take you far away and it'll make many demands. I'll pray for your safety.'

Tolbert sighed. 'You probably need to start praying now.'

Despite Tolbert's comments that had given Dalton the impression that Mitchell was overly pious, Dalton found him to be pleasant company.

Even better, he accepted Tolbert's request that he should look after their cargo without question. He didn't even cast the heavy bundle wrapped in the sheet any over-long looks.

So they dragged the safe into a depression. Then they piled blocks around it to ensure that it wouldn't be visible to prying eyes.

That evening, when they were sitting on one of the shortened chapel walls and eating the meal that Mitchell had provided, Mitchell confirmed in a roundabout way that he would resist the temptation to investigate what they'd brought. He pointed at the pile of blocks.

'Even after my arm's healed,' he said, 'it'll be some months before I sort through those blocks.'

The admission made Tolbert relax, so Dalton took this as his opportunity to pry.

'How long do you reckon it'll take you to rebuild the chapel?' he asked.

'A lifetime,' Mitchell said with a beatific smile that said this wasn't an unwelcome prospect, while Tolbert's steady shake of the head said the opposite.

'That sure is a long time.' Dalton stood and, while holding his tin plate of bread and cheese close to his chest, he considered the blocks and then the chapel wall that was still standing. 'Perhaps there's a way to speed up the process?'

Mitchell's smile didn't waver. 'Speed isn't impor- tant. The Lord will provide and the task will be done when it is done.'

Dalton put down his plate and experimentally shoved the nearest block. It was heavy but, as with the other blocks he had moved, he rolled it on to its end without difficulty.

He then turned to the chapel wall and counted

how many blocks there were in a row and how many rows were needed to reach the required height. He did some quick calculations.

'I figure that if you positioned only one block every day, you could rebuild all four walls on your own in seven years. And if you moved more than one block a day and you got more people to—'

Mitchell raised a hand, silencing him, while Tolbert looked up past the chapel at the rocky peak.

Dalton followed his gaze to consider the silent sentinel. Then he looked at the contented Mitchell, who had also turned to consider the mound.

Mitchell put his plate down and held his hands together in a reverent manner.

'The Lord spoke to me and he gave me this task,' he proclaimed. 'So it is mine and mine alone, as it is the one that shall redeem me.'

'It's yours and yours alone,' Tolbert muttered, 'because you're the only man who's foolish enough to want to do it.'

Mitchell didn't reply, so, before what sounded like a familiar argument broke out, Dalton hazarded a guess at what Mitchell had meant.

'Are you saying you consider yourself responsible for the chapel collapsing?'

'I do.' Mitchell turned to him. 'Because I demolished it.'

'Why?'

'So that I could rebuild it closer to heaven.'

Mitchell came over to stand beside him and all three men looked at the pinnacle. Mitchell's gaze settled on the top of the sentinel before he looked down at the ground and then at the stone blocks.

Dalton peered at the large mass of rock wondering what had interested his partner. As he did so he was able to make out the well-trodden trail that led from the chapel to the base of the rock.

Then he saw the trail that led upwards. He followed it as it spiralled around the monolith, seeing that it had been picked out between and sometimes over boulders.

The rough pathway led up to the summit, which was flat except for a small cairn of stone blocks.

Dalton gulped. 'You're not rebuilding the chapel on the ground; you're carrying the stone blocks to the top of the peak and then rebuilding it there.'

'A lifetime's work,' Mitchell said happily.

'A lifetime wasted,' Tolbert murmured.

'Despite everything,' Dalton said when they were heading back to Fort Lord, 'I don't reckon your brother's loco.'

'Neither do I,' Tolbert said gloomily. 'If only he was, I'd understand him, but I can't think of the right words to describe a man who's dragging a building up a mountain.'

'It's not actually a mountain.'

Tolbert waggled a finger at him. 'Don't make

excuses for him or he might think that what he's doing is normal.'

'Or he might find a real mountain.'

Tolbert winced and held his head in his hands in a show of mock resignation.

'And then I'll have to shoot him in both legs to stop him climbing it.'

'Is that what happened?'

Tolbert sat up straight while adopting a serious expression.

'Yeah, but I didn't plan to do it.'

'I believe you.'

Tolbert smiled, as if Dalton's acceptance of his actions relieved him more than his brother's ready forgiveness.

'I spent every day over the last year trying to talk him out of it. Yet he still knocked down the walls. Then he hammered out a path up to the top of the rock. He kept saying the only way I'd stop him was to shoot him, and one day I got so angry that I did.'

'Don't feel bad. I can see how his plan would annoy you, and he doesn't hold a grudge.' Dalton shrugged. 'The way I see it, your plan to join the cavalry to prove you feel guilty is no less ridiculous than his plan to drag his chapel up that mountain.'

'Perhaps,' Tolbert said, 'and it's certainly more dangerous.'

With that reminder of the unknown dangers they faced, they reverted to silence.

For the rest of the afternoon they concentrated on covering distance quickly so that they could reach the fort by sundown.

Their fears that Arnold might waylay them didn't materialize and they had a quiet journey in which they saw no sign of him or anyone else who was searching for them.

The sun was still low when the fort appeared ahead and, although being away for two days wasn't unusual for troopers, both men were apprehensive about how their unexpected arrival back would be dealt with.

All they knew was that they had to talk to Major Garrison soon and explain the situation.

A mile out of town they saw a straggling line of troopers closing on the town; their mission was unclear. As these riders hadn't been with Arnold's group, Tolbert and Dalton hailed them.

They received a few nods of recognition and they fell in amongst the men as they made their way to the fort. At the gates they were waved on after which they headed across the square.

As neither man saw any sign of Arnold or his troopers, Dalton felt relaxed about the situation. But when Tolbert swung the wagon round to come to a halt in front of the headquarters, the men who had accompanied them stopped thirty yards away and formed a defensive semi-circle.

A row of troopers emerged from the building and

stood in a line before them. Again these men hadn't been with Arnold, but they'd already drawn guns.

Then Major Garrison barked out a command from within the building. In a crisp and efficient manner, they all swung the weapons up together and aimed them at him and Tolbert.

Only then did Garrison come outside to stand before them.

'We've returned with terrible news, sir,' Dalton said, ignoring the guns and facing Garrison. 'We'd like to make our report now.'

'I'll welcome hearing it, Trooper Dalton,' Garrison said, 'but you'll make it from the inside of the stockade while facing a charge of desertion and dereliction of duty.'

'We didn't desert, sir,' Tolbert said as the troopers moved in to seize them. 'We got delayed, but we returned as fast as we could.'

Garrison gestured for them to be disarmed and then taken away.

'Then make your report a convincing one,' he said as hands clamped down on both men's shoulders. 'The last men who told me that story failed. I had them shot.'

CHAPTER 7

'That was an interesting report, Trooper Dalton,' Garrison said. He gestured to the nearest guard, who let him out of the cell.

'And it was the full truth, sir,' Dalton said, although he and Tolbert had been guarded with their version of events.

Being arrested had made them wary of trusting the major, so they'd omitted to tell him of their plan to stash the safe away until it could be returned to Charles. Instead, they'd concentrated on detailing what they knew about Arnold's activities and on explaining how they'd turned against him.

Garrison considered Dalton through the bars.

'Then that proves my plan was the right one,' he said.

Garrison then moved to leave the stockade. Dalton and Tolbert looked at each other and shrugged their shoulders.

'What plan?' Tolbert shouted after him.

Garrison stomped to a halt, conveying with his stiff back that Tolbert shouldn't have spoken to him without respect.

'I put all the rotten eggs in one basket, Trooper North,' he said, swinging round to face them. 'That made Sergeant King become overconfident, except he didn't know that I planned to lead a squad of dedicated men and officers after him. After you left the ranch, I moved in and resolved the problem.'

Dalton cast a significant glance at the deserted jailhouse.

'Then why are we the only prisoners?'

'Because most of Arnold's heathen company fought to the last. I'll give them that.' Garrison frowned. 'But Arnold and several others saved their worthless hides and fled. They're still at large, but I'll track every last one of them down.'

'And Charles Mayweather?'

'Arnold killed him, but thankfully most of his ranch hands survived.' Garrison clicked his heels together before turning to the door. He opened it, but he stopped in the doorway and looked outside. 'I didn't believe a word of your report. Reconsider it, or you'll face a firing squad.'

With that worrying promise, Garrison walked away. Then the two guards followed him out and slammed the door shut to leave Dalton and Tolbert as the only occupants of the jailhouse.

'That threat was just meant to worry us,' Tolbert said after a while.

'I know,' Dalton said with a frown. 'The trouble is, it's worked.'

'It has, but I'm surprised Garrison didn't mention the missing safe.' Tolbert sat on his cot facing Dalton. 'So perhaps he's waiting for us to volunteer that information?'

'Or then again, maybe there wasn't anything in the safe worth stealing?'

Tolbert acknowledged that possibility with a forlorn wince. He flopped down on his cot while Dalton stretched out, again wishing that a few short days ago in another jailhouse he'd stayed in his cell and not tried to help Deputy Rutherford.

That recollection calmed him down by providing the only possible solution to their predicament: doing nothing and letting circumstances dictate their actions.

Tolbert also adopted the same policy, but despite their resolutions to avoid worrying themselves into panicking, the night was a mainly sleepless one and the new day found them restless and pacing their cell.

Throughout the day, they were fed at regular intervals until, after fatigue call, they were taken outside for a one-hour break in a secure part of the fort. At all times, they were watched by their two armed guards along with the other troopers who were patrolling the stockade.

Nobody spoke to them other than to issue brief orders. When incarcerated they saw nobody other than their guards, who acted in a watchful and efficient manner that Deputy Rutherford would have benefited from studying.

Their only hint of what was happening came during their brief time outside, which let them see that few troopers were in the fort as presumably, Major Garrison led the search for Arnold and the rest of the renegades.

This situation continued for the rest of that day and for the next. Before long, a numb feeling overcame Dalton as well as his cellmate and they stopped dwelling on their potential fates.

The days merged into one long, tedious and quiet time with little to distract them or occupy their minds. After a week, they tried testing the guards' resolution with questions about what Garrison was doing.

This only went to prove that not all of the enlisted men had been recruited in the same way as Arnold and many others had. Their questions were sidestepped with ease and the guards returned to their duties quietly, showing that they had no problem with the long hours of doing nothing.

After another week Dalton lost track of the days. The only relief from the boredom came when he and Tolbert exchanged personal histories.

Dalton spared Tolbert none of the uncomfortable details of his early chequered life when the insides of jail cells had been all too familiar. Happily, those years had been followed by better times before it had all been taken away.

Tolbert's tale was broadly the same as Dalton's, of enjoying good times and bad. Most of the bad times involved arguments with his devout brother and the good times had come when he hadn't involved himself in his business.

Eventually, they exhausted the possibilities of their life histories. So then the days passed in near silence, enlivened only by the mundane minutiae of jail-house life.

It was late in the night and they'd broken the day's silence to have a bored debate about whether this was their twenty-seventh day of incarceration or the twenty-eighth when the first activity for a while took place.

The rapid clomping of hoofs out in the square got both men off their cots. They craned their necks and tried to see through the small, high grille in the jail-house wall, this being the only view they had of the outside world.

They could see nothing beyond but darkness, but they found out what was happening soon enough when heavy footfalls approached the jailhouse. Then a line of chained-together troopers was led inside.

They were dirty and bowed, and many sported bloodied scrapes and bandages. One man was unconscious and he had to be dragged in and deposited in a cell.

They were so dishevelled that Dalton remained unsure of their identities until the last man entered. That man was Arnold King; he was the only one to keep his head held high as he followed on after the rag-tag remnants of his company.

While being led to a cell Arnold acknowledged Dalton and Tolbert with only a dazed nod. When the chains of the prisoners had been removed and the cells had been locked, Major Garrison entered.

He stood a few feet in from the main door with his hands held behind him and with his back a little straighter than usual. He considered the full jail-house.

'You nine men are the last of the company that has brought dishonour to the noble traditions of the Plains Cavalry,' he announced. 'The rest got a more honourable and quicker end than they deserved, but for you there is no hope of rescue, no hope of reprieve, no hope other than the redemption you may get in the next life.'

None of the new arrivals responded other than to continue with their groaning as they sought out places to sit that rested their battered bodies.

Garrison ran his gaze over the prisoners. When he looked at Dalton and Tolbert without registering any change in his stern demeanour, Dalton came up to the bars.

'What about us?' he said.

'Now that you've all been brought together,' Garrison said with casual coolness, 'you'll face the firing squad alongside the rest of your associates from hell.'

'But . . . but . . .' Dalton stammered, lost for words.

'I have no interest in your excuses, Trooper Dalton.' Garrison turned to the door. 'You'll all die at sundown tomorrow. Then my troop can begin to prove itself worthy again.'

With that statement of intent, Garrison headed off into the darkness.

Unlike the last time that Dalton had been locked in a jailhouse with Arnold King, this time he wouldn't have minded joining in one of his escape attempts. But Arnold had no secreted knife and no plans in hand.

The only welcome news was that Arnold believed that Dalton and Tolbert had been rounded up in the same way that the rest of the troopers had been caught. From the muttered debates that he overheard, Dalton gathered that Garrison had arrived at Charles Mayweather's ranch shortly after he and Tolbert left and before Arnold had noticed they were missing.

Dalton was unsure whether the possibility that nobody knew they'd taken the safe made it more or less likely that the information would earn them a reprieve.

The next morning, when he and Tolbert discussed their predicament in hushed whispers, they decided that even though they were unsure whether speaking up would work in their favour, it was their only chance. So, when they were fed their morning meal, Dalton told the guard that they had important information for Major Garrison.

As usual, the guard didn't acknowledge that he'd even heard this plea and when he left he gave no obvious signs of passing on a message. Then he stood on guard outside.

When the rectangle of light cast through the grille showed that the sun had risen to its highest point, Garrison had yet to appear. Then the sun began to lower and still nobody came to see them.

Two hours later they got their first visitors in the form of a contingent of guards who led the prisoners outside. Garrison was waiting for them in the head-quarters, but in the bewildering rush of shouting, marching, bugle calls, demands, terse reports and more shouting that followed, they didn't get a chance to volunteer any information.

Only when they'd been returned to their cells did Dalton and Tolbert speak.

'So that was our trial,' Tolbert said.

'Military justice sure is swift and harsh,' Dalton said.

After that the afternoon passed slowly.

As the discontent grew amongst his fellow con-demned men, Dalton would have welcomed a return to the torpor he had suffered for the previous month. No matter how often he called for help, the guards didn't respond; they ignored the other pris-oners' demands too.

With nothing else to occupy his mind, Dalton watched the rectangle of sunlight drift across the floor of their cell and then lengthen when it reached the wall. Every inch it moved brought him closer to an end that now felt unavoidable.

Later, the rectangle grew more diffuse as thin clouds covered the sun, but that only lowered the light level faster and made the end seem imminent even before they were granted the dubious delight of their last meal.

Nobody took up the option.

It was darker than Dalton expected it to be at sundown when a bugle call heralded the guards' coming for them. Although the browbeaten prison-ers showed no signs of offering resistance, there were sixteen guards, two for each man.

Once outside, Dalton saw that even if they had been prepared to fight back, the effort would be wasted as the full contingent of the fort's troopers were stationed outside to witness the executions. The harsh glares they cast at the prisoners showed that, like Major Garrison, they hated Arnold's group for having brought dishonour on them all.

Dalton also saw the reason for the rapid lowering of the light. Ominous thunderclouds had gathered on the horizon, looming behind the row of stakes and providing an appropriately dark backdrop to their grisly end.

The three stakes were set five feet apart and, with nine men to execute, the guards split the prisoners up into three groups. Dalton and Tolbert were placed with Arnold.

Dalton didn't feel lucky when his group was drawn to the back so that they would be the last ones to be lined up at the stakes.

'I'm saving you until last, Sergeant King,' Garrison said, 'so you can witness the deaths of your men and the final failure of your scheming. Then you will die.'

'Don't be so sure I've failed,' Arnold said, raising his chin with defiance as some of his former arrogance returned to his tone. 'I've been stationed here for years. Men who are now standing with you once worked with me.'

'If you've corrupted them, I'll soon make them change their ways.'

'You can try, but can you ever be sure you've rooted out everyone who supports me? Will you ever again be able to trust them to carry out your orders?'

Garrison gave a thin smile. 'In the next few minutes, we'll both find out the answer to that question.'

For long moments Garrison glared at him before he swung away smartly. Then he marched off with a confident stride, leaving Arnold standing slouched and seemingly accepting of his fate after his taunts had failed to chill Garrison's blood.

'Wait,' Dalton said, 'sir.'

Garrison walked on for several paces. Then he stomped to a halt.

'Why, Trooper Dalton?' he demanded with a stern tone that didn't leave room for prevarication even if the situation hadn't been so dire.

Tolbert caught Dalton's eye with a desperate look that urged him to make his plea a good one.

'I have new information that you're not aware of, sir,' Dalton said using a commanding voice that made Garrison turn to him and raise an eyebrow, with approval, Dalton hoped.

'Report.'

'When you arrived at Charles Mayweather's ranch, we weren't there because we were trying to protect his safe from being stolen.' Dalton licked his lips as Garrison's gaze bored into him and made his mouth go dry. 'Acting alone and on our own initiative, we took the safe to a secure place. Then, when we'd completed that part of our difficult mission, we returned here to report to you.'

Arnold joined Tolbert and Garrison in looking at him, his eyes lively with a mixture of surprise and anger. Garrison noticed his reaction and then took a backward pace to appraise the three men.

'Why didn't you report these facts when you faced me the first time?'

'The events at the ranch and your determination to have us arrested on sight made us unsure about trusting you.'

Garrison gave a snort and his eyes flared as he raised his heels to loom over Dalton.

'So you consider me to be an untrustworthy man like Arnold King, do you?' he roared, his voice echoing across the square like a thunderclap from the approaching storm.

'We didn't know the full circumstances back then, but we know now that we were wrong.'

Garrison lowered his voice. 'Then I hope that accepting the error of your ways will give you comfort, even if it won't change your fate.'

Garrison unsheathed the sabre at his hip and started to swing away.

'You have to listen to me,' Dalton shouted, halting the major.

'I don't. Charles's ranch hands didn't mention that a safe had gone missing. I therefore don't believe this latest version of your report.' Garrison raised the sabre and his voice. 'And even now you will call me *sir*, Trooper Dalton.'

'Respect is earned, Major Garrison,' Dalton snapped, anger now taking over from his attempt to gain favour. 'And a man who doesn't listen to his men isn't fit to give orders.'

Garrison flicked the sabre towards him with a motion that was so quick, Dalton thought he'd run him through. But Garrison stayed his hand with the tip held an inch from Dalton's neck.

'Your defiance in the face of imminent death does you credit, Trooper Dalton,' he said, his voice low. 'But for that insult, I'll execute you three first. We shall see if you can keep your courage until the end.'

CHAPTER 8

The twenty paces to the stakes felt as if they were a thousand.

Dalton was determined to walk the short distance unaided. Yet every step required a force of will to raise a foot, swing it forward, and place it on the ground, making him feel as if he were carrying out the act of walking for the first time.

To his right Arnold took his last steps in the manner Dalton expected by shouting threats and abuse, while to his left Tolbert was even more animated. He shook off his guards and embarked on a hopeless attempt to run away, but he managed only three paces before he was clubbed to the ground and then dragged along beside them.

The three men were stood up against the stakes and swung round to face Major Garrison, who then ordered the firing squad to take up positions.

Dalton couldn't bring himself to look at the

shooters nor to listen to the priest who walked by murmuring absolution. So he looked past the men who were standing closest to him to consider the watching men outside the officers' quarters.

These were the only non-military people who had come to witness their demise. They included the judge who had sentenced him along with Sheriff Cleland and Deputy Rutherford.

Garrison stepped back to join them and spoke quietly to the judge. Their easy familiarity suggested that his plan to expose Arnold's activities had been in place for a while.

It also probably explained why the escape from the jailhouse hadn't attracted any repercussions.

Dalton was too worried to ponder on these possibilities. Instead, he did the one thing he'd promised himself he wouldn't do: he looked around for someone or something that would give him hope.

First he looked at Tolbert. He had bowed his head in a show of defeat that Dalton also felt, but which he was trying to avoid showing. Arnold stood defiantly at the stake while glaring around with his feet set wide apart and his arms folded.

Arnold was showing more fortitude than Dalton had expected, so his taunt that he had friends amongst Garrison's other troopers came back to him. With a flash of hope, Dalton looked along the rows of men on either side of the stakes, wondering whether someone might come to their aid.

He saw only cold glares and unconcern for their predicament, but he still refused a blindfold when it was offered, so that he could fight back right up until the end, if an opportunity presented itself.

Arnold also refused the offer and, with a small voice, Tolbert did too. Then everyone moved aside to leave only the firing squad standing before them.

Garrison came forward to stand to the side of the squad where, with the darkness becoming deeper as the storm approached, he wasted no time in delivering brisk instructions.

From the corner of his eye, Dalton saw Arnold tense. He turned to him, hoping that he'd instructed someone to act, but as Dalton himself had done earlier, Arnold had merely raised his gaze to look past the squad at the non-military men beyond.

With even his small hope of a reprieve dying, Dalton followed his gaze. What he saw there made his heart thud.

Deputy Rutherford was no longer with the witnesses. He should have wanted to see the demise of the man who had tried to have him killed, but instead, he was skulking away into the shadows.

Then he disappeared from view, but a few moments later lightning flashed and it presented a brief image of Rutherford standing beside the officers' quarters with a hand on his six-shooter.

The thunderclap came. Its suddenness confirmed the closeness of the storm and made the firing squad flinch before Garrison stood them to attention.

A second flash lit up the square showing Rutherford with the gun half-drawn.

Then the flashes and peals of thunder came in quick succession. During each flash, Dalton caught a brief and stark image of the deputy, and each time his actions became more surprising.

He moved sideways to gain a clearer view of the backs of the firing squad. Then, as the squad knelt to take aim, three troopers on the back row to Dalton's left peeled away and joined him.

Another thunderclap echoed. This time it was quieter than the previous claps and it was closely followed by other rapid claps. But there were no flashes and it was only when a man in the firing squad keeled over on to his chest that Dalton registered that the noises had been gunfire.

Then the rain came.

Water hammered down against the ground, the huge spots splashing up dirt with the promise of an impending deluge.

'Men,' Garrison ordered, waving towards the jailhouse, 'abandon the. . . .'

He trailed off when he noticed the shot man. In an instant, he swung round, seeking out the shooter. His motion encouraged the rest of the firing squad to turn, but that only moved them into the path of the gunfire.

A second man went down clutching his chest and

then a third. That was all the encouragement Arnold needed and he ran forward, pounding across the twenty yards to the shot men as he sought to claim a gun before the troopers could move in on him.

Dalton reckoned that claiming a gun and then shooting his way out of the fort would probably be an impossible endeavour. So he turned to Tolbert, aiming to tell him that they should seek out an alternative, but Tolbert was already moving away from his stake.

'The stables,' Tolbert shouted through the driving rain while pointing. 'Then lose ourselves in the chaos.'

Dalton nodded and ran after Tolbert, putting all thoughts of being shot in the back from his mind as he sought to reach the building where they'd spent their only day of honest toil in the cavalry.

Shouting and volleys of gunfire pealed out from behind as he ran on through sheets of water, which drenched him to the skin within seconds.

The rain cut visibility down to only a few feet, so Dalton concentrated on following Tolbert, the only person he could see clearly, figuring that if he couldn't see far, then nobody else would be able to either.

When Dalton reached the stables he rubbed the water from his eyes. Then, while Tolbert ran towards a stall, Dalton fetched the rigging.

The storm spooked the horses, but Tolbert made a good choice of two relatively calm steeds, and in quick order the two men got them ready to leave.

Elsewhere in the fort the gunfire had stopped, although the troopers were still shouting.

Dalton longed to know what was happening, but he resisted the urge to look outside. When he'd mounted up, with a glance at Tolbert to coordinate their departure, he made for the door.

Once he was outside he was no clearer as to how Arnold's escape was progressing. Even with his hat drawn down low and his head turned away from the rain, the water was hammering down on to the square, which was already under a sheet of water.

Through the deluge he caught glimpses of men running, but they were heading in several directions without any clear aim. From memory alone he turned towards the gates and, with Tolbert at his side, they splashed on through the quagmire.

They'd covered what Dalton judged to be half the distance when lightning flashed overhead giving him a brief image of the gates. To his surprise, they were open.

Men were moving across the open space, possibly seeking to close the gates, but Dalton didn't concern himself with what they were doing and speeded up.

'Keep going!' he screamed at Tolbert.

The stockade loomed on either side as he moved between the gates. Then, a few moments later, he faced the open ground ahead.

'Some are running away and some are riding,'

Tolbert shouted at his side as they turned to head their horses through the town.

Dalton assumed he was referring to the other condemned men, but the change of direction turned him into the slant of the rainfall and water sluiced into his eyes. Temporarily blinded, he couldn't check what Tolbert had meant, so instead he concentrated on keeping moving.

It took him a minute to shake the water from his eyes, by which time he found that they were riding through the centre of town. The jailhouse was to his right and the saloon where his problems had started was to his left.

In his increasingly euphoric state, Dalton couldn't resist waving goodbye to both establishments. Then, with Tolbert at his side, he rode on to the edge of town from where, ahead, the terrain was relatively lighter.

They'd passed the last building when the rain lessened in ferocity. The respite was only partly welcome as, if they could see better, so could their pursuers.

Dalton looked over his shoulder. He saw only the deserted road.

Then, at the other end of town, guards appeared in the fort gateway.

Some men peered uncertainly into the fort while others looked towards town. Then they swung round to face inwards and formed a line to ensure that nobody else could get out unchallenged.

'I reckon they don't know how many have escaped,' Dalton said.

'Yeah,' Tolbert said, 'but they won't take long to figure it out.'

Dalton nodded. 'That means we need to put as many miles as we can between us and the fort before they work out we're missing.'

Now that they'd got used to the light level, the sky towards the horizon didn't seem so bright. Now that the brief storm had moved on Dalton judged that night would come soon.

The ground was muddy; it would mask their tracks so Dalton urged Tolbert to veer away from their current course to confuse the inevitable pursuit. Tolbert used his local knowledge to direct them to a small river that ran into Black Creek.

Then, using a steady mile-eating pace, they tracked along the river until the moon appeared from behind the receding storm clouds. It illuminated the distant town but, to their relief, it didn't reveal any signs of a pursuit.

Their speed and the wind dried them quickly, improving their spirits, and for the next hour they rode away from town, going south at a steady trot.

'If we keep going this way,' Tolbert said after a while, 'it'll be several days before we reach any settlements or any welcoming places where we can hole up. On the other hand, that'll confuse Major Garrison.'

'I like that plan,' Dalton said, and he continued to like it right up until the moment when he saw movement to his left.

He peered into the darkness and, as the moon flitted in and out of the clouds, he caught glimpses of riders moving through the night.

He attracted Tolbert's attention and pointed, but Tolbert returned a sorry shake of the head and pointed in the opposite direction at other riders whom Dalton hadn't seen yet.

The three riders on Tolbert's side were swinging in towards them as, in a coordinated move with the other riders, they sought to capture them in a pincer movement.

Dalton could see no option other than to speed up and try to outrun them, but their steeds were now flagging and the effort seemed doomed to fail.

He was about to slow and seek an alternative direction when Tolbert snorted a laugh.

'They're not Major Garrison's troopers,' he said.

Dalton peered at the rider Tolbert was looking at. This man was now close enough for him to see that he was in fact Arnold King.

Now accepting that they weren't about to be captured, Dalton saw that the other riders were the remnants of his once large squad. There were six riders in total, which was less than the seven men who had faced the firing squad with them.

As Arnold had gathered help in the fort while

they'd been in the stables the battle to escape must have been a ferocious one and it hadn't been a complete success.

This became more apparent when he saw that Arnold's unexpected saviour, Deputy Rutherford, was amongst the group.

'You decided to flee in the same direction as we did, then,' Dalton said when he'd drawn to a halt and the riders had pulled alongside.

'We followed you at a distance,' Arnold said, 'and nobody's followed us yet.'

'I didn't think you trusted us enough to put your fate in our hands.'

'I didn't.' Arnold smirked, his eyes lively in the moonlight. 'But that all changed when you told Major Garrison about the safe you stole from Charles Mayweather's ranch.'

Dalton winced but he hoped his expression hadn't been obvious in the poor light.

'We were trying to talk our way out of facing a firing squad,' he said, speaking with a casual tone to make light of the situation.

Sadly, his words didn't sound convincing even to his own ears.

'I know you were.' Arnold nodded to the riders and they edged apart to surround them. 'But if you don't want us to finish what Garrison started, there'd better be a stolen safe.'

CHAPTER 9

'I don't understand what happened back there in the fort,' Dalton said. 'Last month you tried to kill Deputy Rutherford, and yet he then saved your life.'

'You only need to understand what I tell you,' Arnold King said. 'We may have deserted the cavalry, but you're still under my command.'

Dalton shrugged. Then, as he had asked purely to deflect attention away from himself and Tolbert, he didn't press the matter and returned to warming his hands before the low fire.

An hour after meeting up with Arnold, they had camped in a place that was nothing more than a depression on the plains, but at which a change of horses, clothes and provisions had been left.

The deaths during the escape had ensured that there was enough of everything to go round, and when Dalton had changed out of his conspicuous uniform his mood had improved slightly.

'There's no need to keep quiet about that, Arnold,' Rutherford said, speaking up for the first time. 'I've got nothing to hide now that I've burnt my bridges.'

'You have, but I haven't forgotten that you needed a reminder to make that decision,' Arnold said before he turned to Dalton. 'Rutherford has been taking a cut of our gains, but when I decided to go after Charles's fortune, he wanted a way out.'

'And that was why you threatened to kill him in the jailhouse,' Dalton said. He waited until Arnold nodded before he continued with his surmising. 'But later he relented and burnt down the house to give you an excuse to be deployed?'

Arnold smiled. 'You did well to work that out. If only I could trust you, you could be a useful man.'

'Trust isn't that essential.' Dalton gestured at the men around the fire. 'Major Garrison has always been one step ahead of you. That means somebody you trusted sold you out.'

'Somebody did,' Arnold muttered. 'But I took care of him before Garrison found us. From now on I'll surround myself only with men I trust completely.'

Arnold looked around the small group and they uttered a few grunts of approval. But his consideration of the size of his forces made Arnold lower his head, leaving Rutherford to continue with the conversation.

'So tell us about this stolen safe,' he said, his eyes

bright in the firelight.

Dalton glanced at Tolbert to see which one of them would explain. This time, Tolbert leaned forward.

'We found it in the storeroom at the back of Charles's house,' Tolbert said. 'We were dragging it through the door to take it to Arnold when Major Garrison arrived, so we loaded it on to a wagon and left in a hurry.'

'That's a different story from the one you told Garrison. How do we know you're telling the truth this time?'

'We don't because they're lying,' Arnold muttered before Tolbert could reply. 'Back at the ranch they didn't tell me what they'd found and they left in a hurry because they aimed to keep it for themselves.'

'We didn't,' Tolbert said, not meeting Arnold's eye. 'We explained the situation to the troopers who brought the wagon round to the back. It's not our fault that the message didn't reach you.'

Arnold's eyes flickered with momentary doubt.

'So what was in the safe?' he whispered.

Tolbert took a deep breath while glancing at Dalton, who returned a look of the kind Tolbert had given him in the fort that asked him to make his next statement a convincing one.

'We don't know. It was huge and heavy and it had a secure combination lock on the door. We couldn't open it.'

'That means you tried.'

'Of course.'

Arnold laughed and leaned back to consider them.

'That's the first thing you've said that I do believe. So I might spare your lives.' Arnold raised an eyebrow. 'But only if you show me where you've hidden this safe, with no tricks.'

Tolbert breathed a sigh of relief, leaving Dalton to speak.

'We'll take you to it,' he said. 'But you have to accept that we don't know what's inside. It could be nothing.'

'It could.' Arnold narrowed his eyes as he ended his brief pleasant attitude. 'But if there isn't something in it that makes all this worthwhile, I'll lock what's left of your bodies inside.'

As Arnold was worried that Major Garrison would track them down, Tolbert led the group on a roundabout route to Rocky Point. The journey took two days and they saw no sign of Garrison's troopers, but they all had no doubt he would be scouring the countryside for them.

Dalton learnt that to escape from the firing squad Arnold had employed all the helpers he had acquired from amongst Garrison's men. So everyone who would be searching for them would want them dead.

During those two days Arnold didn't ask about the whereabouts of the safe, trusting that always having at least one man with a gun trained on Dalton and Tolbert would ensure they wouldn't behave foolishly.

In mid-afternoon of the second day of their escape, Arnold worked out where they were going.

'Didn't I hear that you have a brother in Rocky Point?' he asked, looking at Tolbert.

'Yeah,' Tolbert answered cautiously.

'And that you shot him up?'

'I did, but he forgave me and besides, I didn't tell him about the safe.'

Arnold narrowed his eyes. 'Then if he's not guarding it, someone could have found it while you were in the stockade.'

'We hid it well,' Tolbert said without much conviction.

He shot a worried glance at Dalton that said he had the same fear as Dalton had that when they'd left Rocky Point they hadn't expected that they wouldn't return for a month.

With the possibility that the safe might not be lying where they'd hidden it adding extra concern to an already fraught situation, Tolbert stopped seeking out the less frequented routes to Rocky Point. He led them directly there.

Sundown was still an hour away when Dalton saw the monolith ahead, the low sun making it difficult to look at it directly. Arnold drew close to Tolbert.

'Time to tell us where you hid the safe,' he said.

Tolbert pointed at the settlement. 'We stored it underneath the largest pile of rubble outside the chapel.'

Arnold glared at him, conveying that he considered this to be inadequate security. But then, with the resolving to the situation close, he speeded up and drew ahead. His men followed, although they dallied for long enough to cast Dalton and Tolbert fierce glares that promised retribution if they didn't find anything.

Dalton did not quicken his pace, neither did Tolbert, and so when the settlement spread out before them Arnold had a quarter of a mile lead on them.

'Are we going to try to escape while we still can?' Dalton asked.

'You can, but I'm not,' Tolbert answered. 'If the safe has gone, my brother could be in danger.'

Dalton shook his head. 'I'm not leaving you to face this alone. Besides, if it's gone, everyone will be in danger.'

As the two men rode on, Dalton narrowed his eyes and searched for confirmation of whether Arnold had come upon good news or a disastrous revelation.

The first indication that it was more likely to be the latter came when Dalton couldn't find the derelict chapel. He was sure it had been to the west of the settlement, but he couldn't see it. Even though it was possible that in the month they'd been away the one standing wall had collapsed, he couldn't see the rubble either.

He looked at Tolbert, who was staring at the area while worriedly gnawing his bottom lip, confirming that he hadn't remembered the scene incorrectly. They both brightened slightly when Arnold stopped in the right place, but then he and the other riders trampled around aimlessly while peering at the ground.

After covering the area twice, Arnold stopped searching and he turned to face the approaching riders.

'We'd better make the next excuses our best yet,' Tolbert said.

'How can we when we don't know what's happened?' Dalton asked, although he was now close enough to be sure that the rubble from the collapsed chapel had gone.

When they drew up Arnold wasted no time in demanding answers with his firm gaze and several drawn guns.

Neither man could find his voice. So Tolbert orientated himself and then found the depression where they'd stored the safe.

Dalton joined him in jumping down from his mount. Tolbert peered at the dirt, as if by staring he could discern where the safe had gone while Dalton stood back and tried to understand what had happened.

Aside from trampled footprints and a trail of scuffed dirt leading away from the depression, perhaps from the safe's having been dragged aside, he gathered no clues.

Dalton looked up, hoping for inspiration. As he avoided Arnold's piercing gaze, he saw a welcome newcomer heading towards them from the settlement. He feared for Mitchell's life if he was also unable to provide a satisfactory answer, but right now he was their only hope.

Tolbert and then Arnold swung round to face him.

'Brother,' Tolbert said, mustering a cheerful tone, 'I'm pleased to see you again.'

Mitchell no longer wore a sling, but he moved his right arm gingerly as he hailed them with a wave.

'The Lord has provided me with much bounteous joy,' he said, 'and now He brings you back to me.'

'I'm amazed you managed to move the stone blocks so quickly after your arm healed.' Tolbert gulped before asking the important question. 'Did you store our property away somewhere safe?'

'Of course. The safe is . . . safe.' Mitchell smiled as he gestured towards a shack on the outskirts of town. 'It's in my house.'

'Obliged,' Arnold muttered before Tolbert could reply. He gestured for his men to join him as he made off in the direction that Mitchell had indicated.

Only then did Tolbert offer his brother a wide smile and shake his hand. Dalton joined them and the three men stood together to watch Arnold ride on to the house.

'Thank you for not asking any questions about it,' Tolbert said.

'I didn't need to,' Mitchell said. He regarded Tolbert from the corner of his eye. 'I knew whose property it was.'

'Ah,' Tolbert murmured. He kicked at the dirt and looked to Dalton to speak, but like him, Dalton couldn't think of an explanation that would sound plausible while not making them appear as if they'd acted inappropriately. 'This situation isn't as it seems.'

Mitchell dismissed the weak excuse with a shrug.

'I'm not concerned with how you came to be in possession of Charles Mayweather's safe, not on a day that is as welcome as this one is.'

'My homecoming can't give you that much pleasure.'

Mitchell raised his injured arm slowly and patted Tolbert's back.

'Of course it does, brother, but that's not what I meant. Tonight at sundown I will hold the first service in the new chapel.'

Tolbert furrowed his brow, but Mitchell didn't explain. Instead, he raised his eyes to look at the monolith. He moved his head with deliberate slowness as they both followed his gaze. Then he looked up the side of the rocky mass to the summit.

Dalton, shielding his eyes from the low sun, flinched when he saw the flat top. The small chapel stood there, the building now complete. As the walls were the same colour as the rock on which they rested, it looked as if the chapel had always stood there.

'You rebuilt it on the top of the peak,' he murmured, 'in a month.'

'I'd thought it would be my lifetime's work,' Mitchell said with a sigh. 'But I'd also trusted that the Lord would provide and He did. That told me that He had other tasks for me to accomplish.'

'The Lord would provide,' Tolbert uttered in a hollow tone that showed he'd had the same terrible thought as Dalton had. He looked at Mitchell's house, where Arnold was dismounting. 'I hate to ask you this, brother, but is the safe really still in there?'

'Of course it is.' Mitchell rocked his head from side to side. 'But the money that was stored inside isn't.'

'You stole Charles Mayweather's money!' Tolbert spluttered.

'No,' Mitchell said calmly. 'I found a quicker way to complete my task. I used the money to pay a veritable army of men to take the stone blocks up there. They rebuilt the chapel in a month, and on the day the last block fell into place, the Lord certainly looked down favourably on Rocky Point.'

'Let's hope He is still watching,' Dalton murmured as he watched Arnold disappear into the house. 'Because He is the only one who can save us now.'

CHAPTER 10

'But the service won't start for another hour,' Mitchell said as Tolbert hurried him along towards the pinnacle. 'We don't need to go up there just yet.'

'We have no choice,' Tolbert said. 'We've been travelling all day, so we'll never outrun Arnold. That's the only place where we can hole up.'

Mitchell shrugged Tolbert's hands off him and stopped to look up. They were now close to the base of the monolith, from where only the chapel roof was visible.

'You're welcome to attend the first service, but you won't defile a place of worship by fighting.'

Tolbert muttered under his breath. Then he looked at Dalton, shaking his head, silently asking him to explain the danger they were in.

'Aren't you supposed to offer sanctuary to whoever needs it?' Dalton said, trying a different approach.

'I am,' Mitchell murmured in a resigned tone. He continued walking, but this time he moved at a more dignified pace.

Dalton and Tolbert walked behind him. Both men resisted the urge to look over their shoulders until they reached the foot of the steep climb. To their relief, Arnold was still in the house.

'What's Arnold doing?' Tolbert said. 'He must have realized by now that the money's gone.'

Dalton shrugged and he began climbing after Mitchell. He found the going easier than he'd expected. Mitchell had created a path that was wider than it had looked from further away, but the climb was still an arduous one that he didn't think many worshippers would make.

'After I'd removed the money,' Mitchell said when they caught up with him, 'I locked the door. I expect that'll keep him as engrossed as it kept me.'

Mitchell's expression was an inscrutable one. Dalton dismissed the thought that he had acted with more awareness of the consequences than he was letting on.

Tolbert also looked at him oddly, but Mitchell was right: retribution didn't come as quickly as Dalton had feared. Presently, the circular path around the peak took the house out of their view.

Mitchell had tried to turn rocks into steps, but that wasn't always possible and often the climb involved picking out the worn trail between boulders. The higher they climbed, the trickier their footing became and, with the steep sides, one wrong step would result in a quick journey down.

After traipsing along for another ten minutes, the settlement below came back into view. Still there was no sign of Arnold.

The house was now 300 feet below them, so it was possible that when he did come out he wouldn't notice them. Above, the chapel was only a hundred feet away, but the last part of the climb was the steepest.

They formed a line to follow Mitchell's footsteps and pick out the safest route. Even so, they often had to use hands to draw themselves up and, for one section, they had to clamber up with their chests pressed to the rock.

Despite the problems Mitchell had given them, Dalton was impressed with his commitment and, when he crested the top, with the result of his endeavours.

The top of the peak was as flat as it had appeared to be from below; it was only a hundred feet in diameter, forming a rough circle. The small chapel dominated the area and it had been set in the centre.

Dalton and Tolbert hurried on to the nearest wall, where they pressed their backs to it and caught their breath. Tolbert looked skyward while Dalton watched Mitchell approach at a more sedate pace. When he too couldn't be seen from down below, Dalton dropped to his knees and crawled to the edge.

Tolbert joined him and, lying on their chests, they looked down. The first look made Dalton giddy. On the last section of the climb he had looked only upwards, so he hadn't appreciated how precarious a position he was in.

The monolith provided a commanding view of the plains for dozens of miles in all directions, and the settlement below appeared as if it were just a straggling line of discarded pebbles.

When he looked at Tolbert Dalton had to smile. After glancing down for only a moment Tolbert had buried his head in his arms.

'I only ever climbed up here once before,' he murmured with a catch in his throat. 'I vowed then that I'd never do it again.'

'I'll make the same vow,' Dalton said. He gave him a reassuring pat on the shoulder. 'But I can see now why your brother reckoned this place brought him closer to heaven.'

'I know. One wrong step and that's where you'd end up.'

Dalton laughed and, having released some of his tension, he ventured a longer look down. He wished he hadn't, as the ground felt as if it was beckoning him to topple forward.

He had climbed heights before and they hadn't affected him, but they hadn't been as high or as sheer-sided as this place. He gripped the rock to stop himself feeling as if he'd tip over and go tumbling. That calmed him down, but he still didn't like to think about the journey down.

To take his mind off his worries, he picked out Mitchell's house. Nobody was outside except for Arnold's horses; they looked like insects.

'Arnold won't immediately work out that we've come up here,' he said, 'and even if he does, he won't see us unless he braves the climb too.'

Tolbert nodded while still keeping his head buried.

'If he comes up, we need to make it hard for him.' Tolbert shuffled back from the edge for a few feet. Only then did he bring his head up.

Hearing his positive outlook improved Dalton's spirits, although when they'd got back to their feet and returned to the chapel, Mitchell dampened them again.

'I didn't build this chapel so that it could become a place to inflict harm. This is now a—'

'Quit the devout talk,' Tolbert muttered. 'You got us into this mess. You won't stand in our way when we try to get us out of it.'

Mitchell provided a pious smile. 'I only did what the Lord commanded me to do.'

Tolbert set his hands on his hips, now regaining his confidence.

'I don't reckon He commanded you to steal money.'

103

Mitchell considered him with no change in his serene attitude.

'I didn't steal it. I redistributed the money to the needy. Charles Mayweather built his fortune by trampling on others. The people he drove away from their homesteads welcomed the return of their money, and I welcomed their aid.'

With that pronouncement, Mitchell headed into the chapel leaving Dalton and Tolbert to exchange exasperated glances. Then Tolbert followed him in through the doorway that still lacked a door.

Dalton stopped in the doorway while the brothers walked on. When they reached the far end they talked in low, urgent tones suggesting that old arguments were resurfacing.

Dalton looked around the chapel. The inside was a hollow shell, devoid of furnishings aside from four pillars of rock and a slab of stone that stood at the other end. A length of rope was wound around the slab with one end trailing away, suggesting that Mitchell planned to use it to raise the slab on to the pillars and make an altar.

The lack of chairs showed that Mitchell hadn't had enough time yet to complete his work. This also meant there was no food or water available and the chapel would provide only the most basic of shelter on what, this high up, promised to be a cold night.

With his hopes of being able to endure a long siege diminishing, Dalton left the two brothers to resolve their differences. He returned to the edge of the summit where he found that in the last few minutes the situation below had changed.

Arnold's men had emerged from Mitchell's house. Five of them had formed a circle around Arnold – identifiable by his lighter hat – and although Dalton wasn't sure what they were doing, Arnold stood beside an object on the ground: presumably the safe.

They stood for several minutes with only Arnold moving around the safe, making Dalton think that they were debating how to open it. The debate ended when the broad-shouldered Deputy Rutherford and Arnold knelt down beside the safe while the other four men walked away.

One man walked to the horses that Dalton and Tolbert had left and brought them to the house, while the other three headed into the settlement. Despite the distance, Dalton was reasonably sure about what their next actions would be.

First, they searched the town. They were met with opposition, but when confronted, the townsfolk relented and let them look in their houses.

Soon Arnold had confirmed they weren't hiding in any of the obvious places, so his men searched further afield. When they approached the pinnacle, Dalton beckoned to Tolbert to join him.

Tolbert arrived with a pensive expression that showed he hadn't resolved his problems with Mitchell. As before, he didn't look down, so Dalton kept him informed of progress, which for the next fifteen minutes was minimal. The searchers didn't explore the monolith and instead, they searched everywhere else.

The other men milled around the safe, but despite their best efforts it remained closed.

The sun was setting over the distant hills when several townsfolk emerged from their houses and made their way to the monolith. Other riders approached from further afield, showing that despite Tolbert's and Dalton's scepticism, the new location of the chapel had captured some people's interest.

Unfortunately, it also attracted Arnold's attention and he spoke with the first group of worshippers to start on the pilrimage. Their discussion ended with everyone peering up at the chapel.

It was unlikely that those below could see those at the summit, but Arnold gestured and then Deputy Rutherford and another man moved with the townsfolk on to the base of the peak.

'Time's up,' Tolbert murmured when Dalton had explained the situation.

'Will Mitchell help us explain this mess?' Dalton asked.

'No,' Tolbert muttered. He slapped the rock beneath him. 'He won't take responsibility for the effect his actions have on others. All he will do is provide an evening service.'

Dalton shook his head in bemusement. 'He sure is

single minded.'

Tolbert nodded. 'I hope you understand now why he annoys me.'

'I do, but he's still your brother.' Dalton sighed. 'You have to stop fighting with him.'

Tolbert blew out his cheeks and then shrugged.

'Perhaps you're right. I should fight with Arnold instead.' He hefted a stone and then rooted around for a second one. 'There's only one route up here, so we make weapons out of whatever we can find and make it hard for him to get to us.'

Dalton took note of the determined expression on Tolbert's face and nodded. Tolbert found a stone that fitted in to his hand. The weight of it on his palm cheered him, but from behind him Mitchell spoke up.

'If you raise your hand in anger,' he said, 'I'll stand before you and ensure you smite me first.'

Tolbert glared at him, seemingly ready to take that risk. Not knowing how to intervene in this family argument, Dalton looked down.

Deputy Rutherford was now below them on his first circuit. That meant they had ten minutes before he reached the steep section where they could try to fight him off, if Mitchell allowed them to.

On the ground the other four men were standing back from the safe, which now appeared wider than it had before. Then Arnold hurried off to the monolith, shouting at the climbing men.

Dalton couldn't hear his words, but when his angry tone persuaded the men to stop he was able to work out what had happened. He rolled over on to his back to look up at the arguing brothers.

'You'd better decide now whom you're going to smite, Tolbert,' he said.

He pointed down, his worried look encouraging Tolbert and Mitchell to edge forward. Although Tolbert placed a restraining hand on his brother's shoulder when he looked down.

'What's happened to the safe?' Tolbert asked.

'Arnold opened it,' Dalton said. He watched Arnold climb. 'He's not impressed that it was empty.'

'And I reckon,' Tolbert said with a gulp, 'he's now coming up here to complete his promise and stuff our bodies in it.'

CHAPTER 11

'The service will begin in thirty minutes whether these men wish to join us or not,' Mitchell said.

Tolbert glared at him, at last appearing lost for words at his brother's disregard for the perilous situation they faced. Then, with a grunt of anger, he shoved Mitchell aside and marched on to the chapel.

For the first time Dalton fully accepted how Mitchell's attitude had pushed Tolbert into shooting him. He followed after him to walk around the outside of the building, seeking out another option.

Tolbert being unwilling to venture close to the edge, Dalton examined the perimeter of the summit and saw that elsewhere the sides fell away even more steeply than at the place where they had reached the top.

He concluded that there was only one safe way down, but that meant there was only one safe way up, and Dalton faced that conclusion. While he checked on the progress of the men below, Tolbert collected rocks and piled them up.

Unfortunately, Mitchell followed him, tossing the rocks aside as quickly as Tolbert could gather them. This led to more shoving and bickering, so Dalton took it upon himself to gather rocks.

Mitchell didn't try to stop him and Dalton even found three large stone blocks that hadn't been needed to build the chapel walls. He manoeuvred these to the edge to be used as a last resort. Then he piled up the rocks he'd gathered behind his small refuge.

He had cleared the immediate area of anything that could be thrown when Arnold came into view. Arnold had reached the point where the climb became difficult and, without a guide to pick out the safest route, he peered around.

The other men bunched up behind him and cast irritated glances at each other, showing they hadn't been enthused by their journey. The townsfolk who had been climbing to attend the service had grouped together further down; they were in discussion about whether to continue climbing.

Dalton had thought that nothing could stop Mitchell and Tolbert arguing, but when Mitchell noticed that the worshippers had stopped, he stormed to the edge and peered down at the townsfolk with his arms folded.

'The first service will begin shortly,' he hollered.

The townsfolk below showed no sign that they'd heard him, his cry being carried away on the wind, but it made Arnold peer up in bemusement.

Dalton dropped from view before he could be seen. He stared up at Mitchell, torn between wondering whether his intervention would turn out badly or whether it might persuade Arnold to turn back.

'We're not here for no service,' Arnold said from out of Dalton's view. 'We've come for your brother.'

'Then turn back. The only people welcome here are those who come to pray.'

'Does that include Tolbert and Dalton?'

'They are here and while they—'

'That's all I needed to know. Move aside and we'll take care of them.'

Dalton groaned as Arnold muttered orders below and Tolbert even crawled closer to the edge than he had done before to glare up at Mitchell.

'How could you betray us?' he murmured.

Mitchell turned away from his contemplation of the situation below.

'In this place I tell the truth. You can't ask me to do anything else.'

'Then you've got us both killed.'

'I haven't, and maybe if you looked beyond your violent path, you'd find another way.'

Mitchell favoured both men with a benign smile, then turned away towards the chapel.

'If I'm to die up here,' Tolbert said while watching him leave, 'I only ask that I get to throw him off first.'

Dalton didn't bother trying to defend Mitchell; instead he turned his thoughts to the imminent crisis. With their presence now revealed there was no reason to hide. So he edged forward to see that Arnold and the trailing men were now halfway up the steep section and that they were devoting all their energies to the climb.

'It'd be better,' Dalton said, 'if we fought back first.'

Tolbert gave a determined nod and put a hand to one of the three stone blocks. With Dalton's aid, he heaved it forward. He was so angry that he didn't balk at the sight of the drop below.

But once they'd turned the block over the task of directing the misshapen lump towards the climbing men turned out to be harder than Dalton expected. The block resolutely refused to go in the direction they wanted. Then, after the second heave, gravity solved the problem.

The block shifted downwards of its own accord. Then it plummeted over the edge. The two men could only lean forward to watch its progress.

The block hit the rocks ten feet down, making the climbing men flinch and look up. Then it clattered down for another twenty feet where it slammed into a large boulder and went hurtling outwards as it dropped.

It passed Arnold twenty feet to his side and ten feet out from the slope, this being its closest approach to any of the men. Even so they watched its progress until it hammered into another boulder fifty feet down, where, with a heavy thud, it split in two.

'That was just a warning,' Dalton shouted. 'We've got a hundred more blocks up here.'

Arnold drew his six-shooter, but he kept it lowered.

'We've got a slug for every block and I'd prefer a bullet over rocks.'

Dalton couldn't disagree with that taunt, so he spread his hands.

'Either way, we could all die up here fighting over nothing.' He pointed down to the ground. 'The safe had nothing in it.'

'I don't believe you. Give us the money.'

Dalton struggled to find an answer, but luckily Tolbert provided it for him when he pushed the second block over. This time, it needed only one shove to build up enough momentum.

'We've got no money,' Tolbert said as the block toppled over the edge, 'but we've got these stone blocks.'

Arnold didn't retort as he lurched from left to right, trying to avoid the well-aimed block. It careered down on a course straight for him, finding a route that let it turn end over end, seemingly

113

following him no matter which way he moved.

Dalton was sure the block would hit him until, four feet away, it deflected off a boulder and went spinning over his head. Rock splinters cascaded down on Arnold as he was spared his fate, but the man behind him didn't have his luck and the block clipped his right shoulder.

The blow was only glancing, but it made the man shout in pain. He brought a hand up to his shoulder and that unbalanced him. The man toppled over, collided with Deputy Rutherford behind him, who tried to stay his fall. He failed.

Then the man went skittering down the slope, his progress being marked by a prolonged and receding screech of despair until that too was cut off. After he'd silenced, the remaining five men looked down for several seconds. Then, as one, they turned to look up at Dalton and Tolbert.

'You just sealed your fate,' Arnold muttered, raising his gun.

As the other men also drew their guns and swung them up, Dalton wasted no time in drawing back and out of view. Even so, Arnold and the others worked off their anger with repeated gunfire that whined overhead or clattered into the edge of the slope.

Tolbert's brief flash of anger, which had let him overcome his vertigo, had now faded. He sat back from the edge beside their small pile of missiles and the last stone block.

'It looks as if,' he said, 'we'll be joining that man in going down the hard way.'

'If we can stop them reaching the top,' Dalton said, 'we still have hope.'

He hefted a stone and without looking he launched it over the side. An aggrieved muttered comment sounded below, giving him heart and, after a brief discussion about tactics, Tolbert tossed stones over the side while Dalton edged forward with a stone held aloft ready to attempt a more accurate throw.

When he saw the men below they had halved the distance to the top. But a moment later, before he'd been able to throw, Rutherford scythed off a gunshot that cut into the underside of the rock at Dalton's feet and made him jerk back.

So Dalton joined Tolbert in launching a steady rain of rocks over the edge without seeking a target. They didn't repeat their earlier success and all Dalton could hear were grunts of exertion from below as the men got closer.

Within a minute the men were close enough for Dalton to hear Arnold's orders for everyone to spread out, and their stash of stones had all but run out.

With a grunt of anger Tolbert put his hands to the last remaining stone block. With a glance over the side to orient himself, Dalton joined him. They levered it up on to its side and then pushed it towards the climbers.

The moment it toppled over the edge, Dalton leaned forward to follow its progress, but it took an unfortunate deflection. Even though Arnold was only fifteen feet below, the block bounced along getting further away from him with every hit.

'If the other hundred blocks are as badly aimed as that one,' Arnold said with relish, 'we're in no danger.'

Then Arnold put his head down and, with the other men, he scrambled on up the slope. Dalton threw stones down at him. Several found their targets, but with the men staying hunched and presenting their backs to them, the defenders were only rewarded with grunts of pain.

Nothing they did stayed the relentless progress and when Dalton reached down for another stone his hand closed on air. He looked at Tolbert. He was holding the last batch of missiles and they weren't much larger than pebbles.

As the men below started shooting wildly to keep them away from the edge, Tolbert threw the stones over. His downcast eyes said he launched them more out of irritation than because he thought it would help.

Dalton could see that their missiles were gone, leaving them with nothing with which to stop five armed men from cornering them on a rocky peak that lacked any place to which they could run, except for one.

Tolbert batted his hands together, caught Dalton's eye, and then ran for the chapel. With a hollow feeling in his guts, Dalton scurried after him.

CHAPTER 12

When Dalton and Tolbert entered the chapel Mitchell was kneeling down before the altar with his head bowed. He didn't acknowledge that they had entered.

He even appeared to have used the time while they'd been fighting for their lives to try to complete the building of the altar. The rope was no longer attached to the massive stone block and the block itself stood on its side.

The sight made Tolbert mutter under his breath and he turned to look through the doorway. A slug tore into the wall by his right hand causing him to jerk back and making it unnecessary to explain what was happening outside.

'Spread out,' Arnold shouted outside, 'and check around the chapel for other exits.'

This order bought them a few moments and, with time to think, Dalton's gaze rested on the rope, although his mind remained blank as to how they could use it to effect an escape.

'You ready to die with us, brother?' Tolbert asked, not disguising his bitterness in his tone.

'I'm ready for whatever comes,' Mitchell said. He stood and turned to consider them. 'But there's no need for you to meet your end yet, provided you're prepared to turn away from your violent path.'

'I've got no choice.' Tolbert presented his empty hands and batted away the grit. 'All the stones are gone.'

'Then you're ready to accept that my way is the better way?'

Mitchell stood to one side and gestured at the altar.

Tolbert started to mutter something, then he fell silent and, after a shake of the head, he broke into a run. Dalton thought for a moment that he was planning to attack Mitchell, but then he saw what had attracted Tolbert's attention.

When Mitchell had raised the stone slab, it had revealed a hole beneath it.

'How far down does it go?' Tolbert asked Mitchell as Dalton joined him.

'Stop asking questions and get in,' Dalton said before Mitchell could answer.

Dalton jumped into the hole. He then had to jerk aside when Mitchell threw the coil of rope in after him. He crawled on for a few feet beneath the chapel while Tolbert stayed on ground level where, for the first time, he looked at his brother with concern.

'Go,' Mitchell said simply. 'I need to stay to put the slab back.'

'But Arnold will come in at any moment,' Tolbert said, 'and when he doesn't find us here, he sure will be mad.'

'As I've told you, my way is the better way and the—'

'The Lord will take care of you, I know.' Tolbert sighed and jumped down into the hole to join Dalton. He lowered his voice. 'Take care, brother.'

Mitchell didn't reply. Instead, he put his hands to the stone slab. He rocked it until it started to topple. Then, with his legs braced, he lowered it over the hole until the slab proved to be too heavy for him and he released it.

The slab thudded down over the hole with the heavy finality of a coffin lid closing.

The two men were plunged into darkness, making Dalton wish he'd paid more attention to the shape and extent of the hole. He had just started to explore with his hands and feet, finding that the hole angled downwards away from the altar, when rapid footfalls sounded above.

'Where's your brother?' Arnold demanded.

'He left to avoid defiling this place of worship,' Mitchell said with his usual calmness. 'You'll do the same.'

Arnold snorted a laugh. As several others echoed his bemusement, he walked closer.

'You don't order me to do nothing.'

Mitchell didn't reply. Dalton could imagine him standing with his hands clasped before him, favouring Arnold with his calm smile that always infuriated Tolbert. He edged closer to Tolbert, locating him by the faint outline of his form.

'We should see if we can move further away and find somewhere to hide,' he whispered. 'Arnold will soon work out where we've gone.'

Tolbert nodded and shuffled round to move away from the altar. To his surprise, Dalton was able to see these movements with increasing ease as his eyes became accustomed to the darkness.

Only a thin and faint slither of light was slipping under the sides of the altar, so the source of the lightness must be elsewhere and that could mean there was another way out of the hole. Adding further weight to this possibility, a light breeze rustled across Dalton's cheeks.

So, with a growing hope that they might end up somewhere, he crawled on after Tolbert.

After a few yards, he imagined the hole to be a tunnel rather than a hole, and after another few yards he reckoned that the tunnel angled downwards.

'There's no way out of here,' Rutherford's strident voice said above them. 'Where have they gone?'

'Mitchell will tell us,' Arnold said, 'unless he wants to suffer the same fate as his brother will when we find him.'

His voice was some distance behind them, but Dalton noted the menace in his tone, as did Tolbert, who came to a halt forcing Dalton to nudge into his back.

'Keep moving,' Dalton whispered. 'Mitchell may be the most loco, one-tracked fool I've ever met, but I reckon he's the kind of fool who always survives.'

'Yeah,' Tolbert said with resolution in his tone. 'That's because he always passes his problems on to someone else.'

He resumed crawling downwards. Neither man said anything as they shuffled on and, after another few minutes, Dalton reckoned they'd gone further than he'd have expected them to go without coming out somewhere.

He looked back down the tunnel. He judged that not only were they going down, they were also veering to the right. Even though, with every foot they moved on, they were going deeper into the heart of the rocky mound, the tunnel lightened and the breeze wafting past them grew in strength.

The talking back in the chapel also lessened in volume so that Dalton couldn't make out what was being discussed, although the low volume gave him hope that Mitchell wasn't being treated badly yet.

Before long Dalton could see fissures along the

walls that slipped off to the sides. They were all too small to explore, but they suggested that water had exploited weaknesses in the rock.

They found out this was the case when the tunnel took a sudden downwards turn to become a chimney. Dalton shuffled along to stand to Tolbert's side and they peered down.

The drop was around fifty feet. Dalton dismissed using the rope, as he couldn't see anything to which he could attach it, but the chimney was narrow enough for him to press hands to either side. Better still, at the bottom the light was strong enough to be twilight, suggesting they were near the exit.

'I'll go first,' Dalton said.

'No,' Tolbert said with a shaking voice. 'I'll go first. If I think about this, I'll never do it.'

Then, with tentative movements at first, he swung out over the drop and clambered down. Clearly his vertigo didn't affect him when he avoided looking down and he made it to the bottom without difficulty.

He lowered his head to peer at the route ahead, then darted back with a hand to his chest.

'What can you see?' Dalton asked.

'I tried not to look too hard,' Tolbert murmured, then beckoned Dalton to follow him down.

Dalton threw him the rope. Then, picking out the same footholds as Tolbert had used, he manoeuvred himself into the chimney.

He glanced into the tunnel back towards the chapel. Strong light was now illuminating the space and he heard Deputy Rutherford speak, his voice louder than it had been earlier. Then he clambered down.

'I reckon Arnold's moved the altar aside,' Dalton said when he reached the bottom. 'So we need to move on quickly.'

Tolbert clamped a hand over his eyes with an exaggerated look of discomfort and waved a hand in the general direction of the way ahead.

'I reckon *you* need to. I won't be going nowhere.' He peered out between two fingers. 'Unless you tell me it's not as bad as it seems.'

Dalton ducked down into the exiting tunnel to see what had worried his friend. He shuffled forward for four feet to reach the end of the tunnel, then slipped his head through the exit.

The last rays of the sun were lighting up the side of the peak, showing that they had come out on a sheer part of the climb.

'In a way it's not,' Dalton said with a gulp. 'It's worse.'

As Tolbert groaned, he looked down. They had worked their way down further than he'd thought, as the ground was 200 feet away, but there was nothing below for at least fifty feet, and then that was just jagged rocks.

He lay on his side to look up and faced an

overhang thirty feet up.

He remembered traversing that part of the path as even Mitchell had pressed his back to the rock face with concern. Worse, he couldn't remember seeing anything that would snag the rope, even if he could throw it that high.

'Any better news?' Tolbert asked with a catch in the throat.

'None,' Dalton said. 'I can't see no easy way down or up.'

He turned away from his consideration of the bleak terrain outside to face Tolbert, who had at least removed his hand from his face, although he'd fixed his gaze resolutely on a point in the distance.

Dalton took the rope off him and laid it down at his feet. He counted the coils of rope to judge its length, coming to a figure of about forty feet.

Then he glanced around looking for a place to snag the rope. He saw none and so, with a wince, he returned to measuring the rope hoping to make a better judgement of its length while also avoiding catching Tolbert's eye.

'There's a better way,' Tolbert said in a hollow tone, 'to work out if it'll reach whatever's down there.'

'I know,' Dalton murmured. 'I was just trying to avoid getting our hopes too high before I see if it reaches down to the bottom of the steep section.'

Tolbert patted his shoulder. 'You weren't, but

don't worry, we both know how we can secure the rope at this end.'

Dalton reached the end of the rope and then looked at Tolbert.

'I know.' He sighed. 'Is there no other way?'

'Not even Arnold King and his men coming down the chimney with their guns a-firing could get me out there on the end of that rope. So I'll hold one end and you go down. Then see what you can do to help me and Mitchell.'

Dalton slapped the ground in irritation. 'This situation just can't get no worse.'

The two men sat in silence for a few moments until, with a cough, Tolbert pointed past Dalton's shoulder.

'Except it can,' he murmured.

Dalton turned and peered across the plains. In the distance riders were kicking up dust, the vast plumes masking their forms, but there were undoubtedly dozens of them.

'Who?' Dalton murmured, although with a sinking feeling in his gut he worked that out before Tolbert could reply.

'Major Garrison,' Tolbert said. 'The only man who wants us dead more than Arnold King does.'

CHAPTER 13

Major Garrison had made camp at the base of the peak.

As dusk had now closed in his fires were bright and, in a welcome piece of good fortune, his arrival had slowed the progress of Arnold's men. People were still talking in the tunnel above, but others had returned to the top.

So Dalton and Tolbert had also stayed quiet in the hope that Garrison didn't know they were here. This became increasingly likely when he didn't explore the vicinity and the brief conversations some of the troopers had with the townsfolk didn't appear to add urgency to his activities.

'It's decision time,' Dalton said, peering at the diminished arc of light on the western horizon. 'It'll soon be too dark to risk moving on.'

'Arnold won't make a move until it's light tomorrow,' Tolbert said, 'so that'll give you until sunup to do something, except I don't know what.'

'I won't be able to figure that out sitting up here.' Dalton picked up the rope and tossed it to Tolbert. 'So wish me luck.'

Tolbert nodded. Then he looked around for a secure position from which he could take the strain while Dalton lowered himself down.

Dalton fashioned an end into a noose to wrap around Tolbert's chest. Then, without further comment, Tolbert took his end and braced his feet against a protruding rock while Dalton shuffled on to sit on the edge with his feet dangling.

He checked that Tolbert was ready. Then he threw the rope over the side and caught his boot on a small protruding rock. He lowered himself into the gloom.

With a murmured prayer for luck, he swung round to place his feet to the rock. After several deep breaths, he set off down the sheer rock face.

Quickly, he found an efficient rhythm of walking while he played out the rope. When he looked up he was delighted to find that after only a few paces the tunnel entrance had disappeared into the gloom.

So he looked down, but the news wasn't so good. He couldn't make out the rocks below and he was sure he could see the dangling end of the rope.

He shook himself to banish negative thoughts and, while he still felt strong enough to get down and then back up again, he continued clambering downwards. Every few feet he checked that rope was still below, but faster than he'd hoped, he approached the end and still he couldn't see a safe place below.

He slowed his progress and looked around, hoping to see something to either side that he could reach, but the sheer rock face vanished into the darkness with no suggestion of there being ledges on which he could rest.

A few paces further on he ran out of rope.

Standing sideways with his feet planted firmly and one hand on the very end of the rope, he looked over his shoulder at Garrison's camp. The troopers who were outside were around 300 feet away from the base of the peak. Nobody showed any sign of having seen him, but then they had no reason to look up.

Then he looked straight down and narrowed his eyes, hoping to see something below, but he saw nothing other than the sheer wall. He conjured up an image of the scene while it had been light, but back then, from his different perspective, the end of the sheer stretch had appeared closer, and worse, the rocks below had been jagged.

He wriggled, hoping that it might get him a little closer. To his surprise he dropped down for a few feet. Thinking he'd freed trapped rope, he repeated the motion; he moved down again.

A strangulated screech sounded above and, with a gulp, Dalton realized what must have happened. The strain of holding him up was taking its toll on

Tolbert's arms and he was slipping forward.

'Are you all right?' Dalton said in an urgent whisper.

He strained his hearing and made out muttering coming from above. Then he dropped another foot, then another, in sharp movements that told him everything he needed to know about the struggle Tolbert was having up in the tunnel.

He bent his legs and swung closer to the rock, hoping that he might find purchase and so lessen the strain on Tolbert's arms, but his boots slipped on the smooth surface. Again he slipped down, and when he looked up he saw movement briefly as an object flashed and then moved out of view back into the tunnel.

He wasn't sure what he'd seen, but he presumed that Tolbert's clothing had caught the light before he'd struggled back into the tunnel. He looked down, but he could see nothing below on which he could land.

Dalton had perhaps just seconds available before the strain became too much and his weight dragged Tolbert out of the tunnel. He risked calling to him, this time louder. Only a grunt of effort sounded, and then he dropped, this time for several feet before he fetched up again.

He reckoned that that movement might be his last one before Tolbert fell. He scraped his boots down the rock until he was dangling one-handed from the bottom of the rope.

He cast a last look down, seeing nothing below. Then he opened his hand.

For one heart-sinking moment he fell. Then he crunched down on hard rock and pitched to the side. He threw out a hand, hoping to stay his progress, but his fingers merely brushed rock and then he was falling again.

This time the fall lasted for longer and he descended through the darkness with no feeling that it would end. Then he hit something.

He heard a sickening crack. The darkness spread and consumed him.

Dalton opened his eyes.

It was dark. Time had passed and something was wrong. For some reason that he couldn't grasp he didn't want to work out what the problem was.

As he was lying face down in the dirt, he moved his head into a more comfortable position and, unbidden, a groan escaped his lips. Then, as if that movement had triggered an awareness of his body, pain arrived.

First his forehead throbbed, and then his right arm. Then aches and bruises announced themselves all over his body.

He acknowledged each new source of pain with a groan, but also with a sense of relief that he had somehow survived the fall. The grit beneath his hands and the solid mass that lay beneath his chest and legs told him he could have tumbled all the way to the ground.

He narrowed his eyes. It was too dark to see the terrain in his immediate vicinity, but after a minute he discerned glows of light ahead. He had to strain his neck to see their extent.

His returning senses told him that these were the fires in Garrison's camp and that, as they were level with him, he must be on the ground. He decided to sit up and take stock of his situation.

He didn't move.

He tried again, pushing off with his feet and twisting. This time he moved, but the effort sent hot fire coursing up his legs and then into his back and, strangely, into his head.

He couldn't avoid screaming. To his relief the sound emerged only as a croak, so he fought to keep his mouth closed and pressed his forehead to the dirt, willing the pain to pass.

It didn't.

With seemingly no end to the torment, he strained his hips and succeeded in rolling over on to his back, where he tried to work out what he had done to himself. The new position relieved the agony slightly. Looking up at the stars, he took deep breaths until by degrees the pain receded from his upper body and returned to his legs, where it had started.

Experimentally, he moved his left leg. He found

that he was able to raise it without pain, so, with a gulp, he tried to raise his right leg. A bolt of pain tore up his leg, into his chest, and all the way to his head.

This time the pain receded quickly, reverting to just a dull throb. He steeled himself and looked down.

He wished he hadn't. He laid his head back down on the ground and looked at the stars.

'It's not meant to be at that angle, Dalton,' he murmured.

He felt his thigh and then worked down to the knee, finding that they didn't hurt before he risked looking again at the lower leg. It was as bad as he'd feared from the first glance.

After that, he couldn't bring himself to look at the leg again.

Time passed. How long, he wasn't sure, and he couldn't make plans because there didn't seem to be anything he could do.

Instead, he fixed his gaze on a bright star that was above the mass that stood darkly before him and which must be the monolith.

He watched the star edge closer to the mass until it disappeared. A few moments later it reappeared letting him see that it had brushed behind the chapel roof. Then it disappeared and didn't reappear.

That sighting helped him to orient his position and pick out the spot where he reckoned Tolbert would be, provided he hadn't fallen too. Considering his friend's predicament helped him to take his mind off his own misery and forced him to think.

The settlement was on the other side of the monolith; a short journey on foot, but an epic trek when one foot wasn't pointing in the right direction.

He gulped down a wave of nausea as an image of his lower leg came back to him. Then, as much to stop himself dwelling on this as anything else, he dug his hands into the dirt and pushed backwards.

He moved for a few inches and, even better, the movement didn't add to his discomfort. Pleased at this positive action, he repeated the motion. Slowly, he edged his way along.

After a while he experimented with various positions until he found that lying on his side and kicking backwards with his uninjured leg while clawing his way on with elbows and hands worked best. He maintained this motion, moving on towards the light.

Presently the light grew brighter and he heard movement. Then someone spoke up. The words were uttered too low for Dalton to hear, but the tone said a question had been asked, presumably about the noise he was making.

Dalton stopped moving and considered, but only for a moment as, without the distraction of moving himself on, his broken leg started throbbing with greater insistence, the waves of pain matching the speed of his racing heart.

'Over here,' he said; then, having made the

decision to put his fate into the hands of a man who would probably have him shot on sight, he raised his voice. 'I'm over here.'

For a while silence greeted him until, with a sudden burst of movement, two troopers appeared, having clearly sneaked up on his position expecting deception. They trained guns down on him, so Dalton raised one hand while waving the other hand weakly at his leg.

'Hurt, bad,' he groaned.

One trooper glanced at his leg and winced. Then he hurried off to fetch help.

The other man kept his gun on him and said nothing. That was fine with Dalton and he concentrated on keeping his thoughts elsewhere through the next few uncomfortable minutes.

Two men arrived with a stretcher. He was dragged on to it and then taken into the camp. The people he saw didn't show any signs that they recognized him and they didn't ask for his name.

Dalton didn't volunteer one, not that he was in the mood to talk, although he did entertain the hope that maybe he wouldn't be recognized and then, after being treated, he might find a way to help Tolbert.

To his relief, when he next considered his surroundings, he realized that he was lying on a low table within a tent and a man whom he recognized as being the troop's surgeon was appraising him with a practised eye.

'I've got good news and bad news about your leg,' he said with a jovial gleam in his eye that spoke of his years of putting injured men at ease.

'I hope the good news is that'll be all right,' Dalton said.

'It is, except the bad news is: this'll hurt.'

'Just do what you have to do.'

The surgeon beckoned and three men moved in. Two men held his shoulders while another held his legs down above the knees. A leather strap was thrust into his mouth and he was told to bite down on it.

Dalton did as ordered and tried to put his mind elsewhere again. He looked beyond the men surrounding him.

His gaze picked out the one man who wasn't working on him. Dalton looked him in the eye; he'd been so successful at distancing himself from proceedings that at first he didn't recognize him.

Then he saw that the man was Major Garrison. And he was smiling.

He had just enough time to return an ironic smile of his own. Then the surgeon grabbed his ankle in his firm grip and pulled.

CHAPTER 14

'Have you stopped vomiting yet, Trooper Dalton?' Garrison said, kneeling down beside Dalton's low cot.

'I've got nothing left to give,' Dalton murmured. He rubbed his lips with the back of a shaking hand.

Garrison leaned back to appraise his leg.

'Then the pain was worth it. He made a good job of your leg.'

'Yeah. It doesn't hurt so much no more.'

In truth he had only ventured a glance at the leg to confirm that it was now straight before he'd lain on his back on the cot to await whatever fate Garrison had in store for him.

'I'm pleased. A man should be able to face the firing squad with all his faculties intact.'

With a sudden burst of anger, Dalton slapped a hand on Garrison's wrist. Garrison considered the hand with contempt, but he made no move to shrug him off, so Dalton fixed him with his gaze.

'You got Tolbert and me all wrong,' he said.

'I know men like you, Trooper Dalton. I don't think so.'

'Then amongst your other failings, you're not the judge of character you reckon you are. Tolbert and me were both victims of circumstance. Arnold almost killed us on our first night in the fort and nobody came to help us then. So we had no choice but to stick together. We spent our few days in the military trying to stay alive.'

'I believe you.'

'And . . .' Dalton trailed off when Garrison's comment registered. 'So why are you determined to have us shot?'

'Because you lied to me, Trooper Dalton. If you'd reported the full truth when I first arrested you, I'd have believed you and had you thrown in the stockade for a week for dereliction of duty. But your tale made no sense.'

'Sometimes the truth doesn't, but since we left the fort, we've been doing your job for you and taking on Arnold.'

'So where is he?'

Dalton raised his hand from Garrison's wrist and pointed in the direction he thought the monolith would be.

'He's holed up on the top of that rocky peak where I reckon he's keeping Tolbert's brother hostage, while Tolbert is in hiding up there too. I escaped and came down to warn you and to get your help, except I fell and broke my leg.'

'And the safe?'

'I . . .' Dalton glanced away to collect his thoughts. When he looked back Garrison had narrowed his eyes.

'And there's the problem, Trooper Dalton. You're hiding something, even now.'

'Perhaps I'm thinking of others, not myself.'

'Perhaps you are, but it's not the duty of a trooper to think. He leaves that to his commanding officer.'

Garrison gave Dalton a long look before he stood and walked towards the tent flap.

'And so what happens now?' Dalton shouted after him.

'You,' Garrison said in a quiet voice, 'have to decide whether you're prepared to call me sir.'

Garrison slipped outside, leaving Dalton to lie back on his cot. He couldn't tell whether Garrison had offered him a way out, but he willed himself to relax in the hope that he could lessen the soreness.

Now that his major source of pain had been dealt with, his whole body felt battered, as it should do after he'd tumbled half of the way down the monolith.

He tried, as he'd had to do in the stockade but had failed to do in the jailhouse, to accept that his fate was no longer in his own hands. To his surprise this must have worked as, seemingly a few moments later, it was light outside the tent and with a tentative stretch he saw that he must have fallen asleep.

In the distance a bugle sounded and a man shouted. Dalton strained his hearing and he heard more shouting, the tone sounding as though orders were being delivered. As this wasn't an unexpected happening in a military camp, he tried to dismiss the flurry of anxiety about whether Garrison had decided to take on Arnold at first light.

If he had, the size of his troop ensured that he would prevail. Dalton could only hope that Tolbert and his brother managed to survive whatever Garrison had planned.

Dalton shuffled on his cot, finding that his leg was comfortable. So, dismissing his previous thoughts, he gripped the side of the cot with one hand and, with the other holding his thigh firmly, he lowered himself to the ground with care.

A dull thud sounded when his leg touched the ground, showing that it had been well splinted. So he judged that as long as he was careful, he could avoid hurting himself when he moved.

As he had done late last night, he crawled along on his side until he reached the tent flap, accomplishing the journey in three relatively painless movements. The scene outside was not as he'd expected it to be.

At first, he couldn't see any troopers. He moved on

for a few yards, and that let the rest of the camp come into view. Two guards were standing in broadly the positions they had taken up last night facing the monolith, but they appeared to be the only men here.

Dalton sat up and from the higher position could see that the camp had been abandoned. He soon saw where they had gone.

Troopers were moving over the climbable parts of the monolith like ants on an anthill and, as with ants their actions appeared unfathomable even when you knew that they must have a purpose. Some men were moving upwards and some were moving sideways while others stayed put.

After a few minutes Dalton concluded that they were seeking to reach the summit and catch Arnold by surprise and that they were doing so by avoiding the obvious route up. Presumably Arnold was guarding this path.

There was nothing Dalton could do to help this assault. But he set off anyhow.

Moving as slowly as the men climbing the monolith, Dalton edged his way along, slipping between tents to keep out of the sight of the guards. Then he took as wide a detour as he could manage around the monolith.

By the time he'd moved for fifty yards out of the camp and he was starting to think he'd avoided being seen by the guards, the sun was poking out above the distant mountains.

He kept moving until he faced the main route up, at which point his broken leg was protesting with an insistent throb, forcing him to rest in a hollow. He adopted a position lying on his back to keep his leg stretched out straight. Then he tried to make sense of what was happening.

From this position he couldn't see any of the troopers. That observation made it clear that Garrison was seeking to keep the main path free.

Dalton was considering whether he should turn back when he saw movement high up on the monolith. He narrowed his eyes, and when he picked up the movement again he saw that several men were making their way down the main path. They weren't wearing troopers' uniforms.

As he could be seen from high up, he dragged himself out of the hollow and to the base of the monolith, urgency now forcing him to risk pushing himself on at greater speed. He didn't waste time checking on what was happening above and, within two minutes, he reached the first straggling pile of boulders on Mitchell's path.

Gratefully, he crawled into cover. He had just flopped down on to his back when a long shadow spread over his face making him flinch. A moment later Major Garrison peered down at him.

'Crawling around on your belly like a snake,' he said, 'and disobeying orders again, are we, Trooper Dalton?'

Dalton mustered a smile. 'I sure am.'

Garrison snorted. 'And still you struggle to call me sir.'

Dalton shuffled backwards to lean against the boulder.

'Men are coming down the main path. They'll be here in about ten minutes. The final length of path to the ground is steep, so they'll be at their most vulnerable then.'

Dalton found that he couldn't end his report in the way Garrison wanted him to. This mattered to Garrison, so, in a strange way, in a situation where the major held all the high cards, Dalton had gained a small advantage over him.

'I'd already worked that out,' Garrison said. 'That's why I deployed men in the positions I chose, and they'll follow my orders.'

'And what are your orders for me?'

'You don't have any, Trooper Dalton. You're under arrest.'

Garrison started to turn away, but Dalton coughed, making him turn back.

'Except you didn't put a guard on me.'

Garrison considered him, but his impassive gaze didn't waver before Garrison took up a position where he would be able to see the path while remaining hidden from up above.

'I am guarding you, Trooper Dalton,' he said. 'Make one move to alert your friends and I'll deliver

143

summary justice right here.'

'I only care about two people up there.' Dalton paused, finding to his surprise that despite his odd behaviour he did care about Mitchell's fate. 'If they're in danger, I'll do what I have to.'

Garrison looked over his shoulder to consider him.

'So you, unarmed and unable to walk, will step in on your one foot and help your fellow deserter and accomplice in stealing the safe, will you?'

'I will.'

Garrison shook his head and resumed looking at the path. Dalton waited for him to continue their conversation, but when he didn't, he registered what the major had just admitted for the first time. He believed they had taken the safe, and he probably also knew that it had once contained a lot of money.

As it was also likely that he wouldn't be as determined as Dalton was to ensure that Tolbert and Mitchell survived, Dalton took stock of his physical state. With his back braced against the boulder, he flexed his thigh and then tried to raise his broken leg.

He couldn't make the leg move and a grunt escaped his lips, making Garrison wave at him to be quiet. Dalton rolled on to his side. Then, again dragging his leg along behind him, he moved to sit beside Garrison.

The major cast him an irritated glare, but he said

nothing; the reason became apparent when footfalls sounded higher up on the monolith as, presumably, Arnold made his move to leave. Dalton heard low rustling as, from out of his view, other nearby troopers edged into position.

Dalton tried one last attempt to raise himself, but when that failed, he accepted that he had to put his faith in Garrison. He sensed Garrison twitching with anticipation. Then the major leapt to his feet.

'You're surrounded,' he proclaimed, brandishing his gun. 'One wrong move and you'll all die.'

'You showed your hand too early,' Deputy Rutherford said from out of Dalton's view. 'Stay back.'

Dalton moved so that he could see Garrison's expression and gauge his reaction, but other than a firming of the chin, he gave no hint as to whether he would call Rutherford's bluff.

'A man who abused everyone's trust doesn't give me orders.'

Rutherford laughed. 'I do, because just us two have come down. Everyone else stayed up there. If you try to stop us leaving, Arnold will shoot the hostages. So the only question is, are you prepared to see five innocent men die.'

'Five?'

'Mitchell North's service last night attracted the townsfolk, after all. They soon wished they hadn't come. So, are you prepared to negotiate, or do we start killing them?'

Garrison didn't answer but, his gaze being set on Rutherford, Dalton didn't wait to find out the answer. He lowered his upper body to the ground. Then he started dragging himself along.

He'd managed to move several body lengths before he stopped to catch his breath. Garrison was still facing Rutherford, who was out of his sight. He looked up.

The monolith loomed for hundreds of feet above him, the path being a hard enough climb on two legs. Dalton rubbed his elbows and flexed his arms. Then he set off.

CHAPTER 15

Dalton was fifty feet above ground when his flagging strength finally gave out.

He lay on his side and looked down the slope, feeling amazed when he saw how far he'd dragged himself using sheer willpower. Down below Major Garrison and Deputy Rutherford were facing each other while the other man who had come down with Rutherford looked around for deception.

They were talking, presumably about the deal Rutherford was trying to broker. Garrison didn't appear to have registered that Dalton had left, but whether that showed that he approved of his actions, he couldn't tell.

On the way up he had kept away from the path and had picked a route which, until now, had kept him hidden from down below. Neither had he seen the other troopers, who were no doubt sprawled about around him.

On his back Dalton looked up at the remainder of the route to the top. He figured that even if circumstance gave him the time and his strength held out, it would take all day. Worse, from here on the only route up was the path that Mitchell had carved out.

Even though sweat from his exertions dampened his clothes and his arms shook, he got back into position for the next stage of the journey. But then Rutherford looked up and the deputy beckoned to someone who was in a higher position than Dalton.

Dalton stayed still. Presently Rutherford turned back to face Garrison, suggesting that Dalton had avoided detection. That narrow escape made him accept that he'd done everything he could for now.

He shuffled on for another few feet and picked a position where he could lie behind a low boulder from which he reckoned he couldn't be seen from the path, but which would let him act if someone came close to him. He waited for Arnold to come down.

As it turned out, he had to wait for an hour.

Garrison left the monolith to give orders and Arnold's horses were brought to its base along with four others. As one man had fallen off the monolith, this meant that Arnold planned to take all the hostages with him, showing he knew that just taking Tolbert and his brother might not stop Garrison from confronting him.

Then they all waited. Dalton strained his hearing

as he listened out for Arnold and the others approaching. Listening helped to take his mind off the stark fact that he had no idea what he could do when they passed him.

The most likely thing that would happen was that he would be seen. This would add to Garrison's problems while possibly putting the hostages at risk. That thought helped to batter down the bravado that had made him leave his sick bed and drag himself up here.

He looked around for a place in which he would have a better chance of avoiding detection. Eventually he settled on making for a gap between two boulders. While keeping his head down, he crawled along, seeing that the gap opened up into a wider space, but he still judged that nobody would be able to see him there.

He put his head down and dragged his body on for two more pulls. Then he looked up, only to find he was staring down the barrel of a six-shooter.

'What are you doing up here?' the gun-toting trooper muttered, keeping his voice low.

'Same as you,' Dalton said. He nudged the gun aside with his cheek and moved on.

The trooper didn't try to stop him and behind him a second trooper moved into view. This man took his shoulders. Gratefully, Dalton relaxed and the man helped him to slip into the gap.

He lay in the shade in the narrow gap, where he

saw that the two troopers were bedded down between two flat-topped rocks, from where they were in the perfect position to stand up and mount an assault.

Dalton started to ask them what their orders were, but a downward wave from a trooper silenced him.

Then he heard people approaching. Mindful of his latest resolution not to make things harder for Garrison's men, Dalton took hold of his leg and dragged it round to place it sideways across the gap.

This new position let him see troopers moving between rocks further down the slope. Unfortunately, Arnold must also have noticed them, for his voice rang out clearly.

'It's a trap! Turn back.'

Rapid footfalls sounded. The two troopers adopted a crouched position so that they could look over the low rocks. They picked out targets, then splayed rapid gunfire.

Returning shots rattled away, but they must have been directed at other troopers, as the two men beside Dalton remained in their raised positions.

The man nearest to Dalton quickly regretted that decision when he went spinning away clutching his shoulder. His gun flew from his grasp and clattered down on to the rock in front of him.

The second trooper glanced at him and then, with a roar of anger, he put a hand to the rock and vaulted it. Several shots rang out, but he had moved from view, so Dalton was unsure of his fate.

But he had seen where the first man's gun had fallen.

He shuffled around to place his back to the boulder facing the path, then slapped a hand on the rock and used it to claw himself up. The wounded man watched his movements while shaking his head in bemusement before the pain got the better of him and he lay down on the ground.

Dalton noted that he was breathing shallowly. Then he used his uninjured leg to give him extra impetus and, in a sudden burst of movement, he rose up and sprawled over the boulder facing the path twenty feet ahead.

The scene was largely as he'd imagined it: the precarious nature of the path constraining the actions of the men working their way down the monolith. Arnold was walking behind Mitchell and Tolbert. He had a hand on Tolbert's shoulder keeping him in a position where he could use him as a shield. Deputy Rutherford was hurrying up towards them.

Arnold's other men were spread out along the path. Several of them had fallen, while the hostages had knelt down, appearing unsure which direction would give them a chance of reaching safety.

Dalton rooted around on the top of the flat rock for the gun the man had dropped. He saw it lying a few feet beyond his grasp at the far end of the rock. He braced himself, then kicked off with his good leg.

151

His fingertips brushed the gun. Unfortunately, his efforts sent the weapon skittering even further away, after which it fell from view on the other side of the rock.

Dalton groaned in irritation and strained to move himself on, but he was already on tiptoe on his good leg and he could go no further. He looked up to find that Tolbert had been turned round to face him; he was staring at him with a mixture of surprise and relief.

Arnold wasn't paying him any attention as he sought to keep his back to the slope so that he could face the troopers. Dalton spread his arms across the rock, seeking purchase. He found none, and worse, he started slipping backwards.

For a moment he almost gave up and accepted that he could do nothing to help Tolbert, but the movement placed his full weight back on his uninjured leg. So with a grunt of effort he flexed his leg and then kicked off.

He went sliding forward on to the top of the rock. Then his momentum kept him moving on until his head was pointing downwards. He was seeking to stay his progress when he saw the six-shooter lying on a ledge on the other side of the rock.

He slapped a grateful hand on the gun as he slid uncontrollably onward. He threw out his other hand to cushion his fall, but the movement jarred his broken leg and sent a bolt of pain shooting up his body, making him go into spasm.

The next he knew he was lying awkwardly on the ground with his shoulders pressed to the dirt and his legs propped up on the rock above him. He tried to shuffle round to lie more comfortably, but his limbs refused to obey him.

Then, slowly at first, gravity took over and dragged his legs down the side of the rock until with a clatter they both landed on the ground. A sharp pain sliced through his leg. Again Dalton lost control of his body and lay twitching.

Somewhere close by sounds of an argument broke out, dragging his senses back to wondering what was happening to the others.

'Take me,' Mitchell said, his voice rising above the growing hubbub. 'Not him.'

'No!' Tolbert shouted.

Clearly the situation was coming to a head, so Dalton gritted his teeth and willed himself to move away from his constricted position.

With his head lowered, he walked his free hand along the ground until it reached a small boulder. This he used to lever himself up to a sitting position. This position relieved the pressure on his broken leg, so he continued pushing until he was kneeling on his good leg and his bad leg was pushed out sideways.

He steeled himself and then tried the one motion that he had thought would be beyond him. With his weight on his hand he drew his knee up and then straightened his good leg.

When he next looked up he was standing with his weight on his good leg and his gun held downwards. Six feet before him stood Mitchell with his arms spread wide, protecting Arnold as if he welcomed anyone taking a shot at him.

Tolbert was at his feet, having been pushed aside; he was edging himself along to one of Arnold's fallen associates, presumably seeking to wrest a gun off him. Arnold would notice him soon and, reckoning this might give him the distraction he required, Dalton straightened his posture as much as he was able. Then he levelled the gun on Mitchell, who caught his eye and smiled.

'Do it,' he said; then, when Dalton didn't react, he shouted, his voice echoing amidst the rocks. 'Do it!'

Dalton shook his head and stayed his fire, waiting for an opening. Mitchell again shouted his demand; this time Arnold looked over his shoulder and saw Dalton standing before him.

He flinched with surprise just as a gunshot tore out from one of the troopers, making Mitchell scream and then slump forward, his body a dead weight in Arnold's grasp.

That was the moment Dalton had been waiting for. He blasted a gunshot that was ill-directed but which still caught Arnold's gun arm a glancing blow. The shot made him spin round and release Mitchell, who fell at his feet.

Their movements revealed Rutherford. He was swinging his gun round towards Tolbert, but Dalton tore off a quick shot that hammered low into the deputy's stomach before he could fire, making him double over and fall to his knees.

A moment later Dalton also fell, the strain of levelling his gun and shooting proving too much for his precarious one-legged stance. He toppled sideways and, while turning his gun back on Arnold, he squeezed out another gunshot; it flew several feet wide of its target.

Then he fell without control. Arnold followed his progress with steady assurance.

A gunshot tore out, the sound loud and coming from close by as Dalton landed like a felled tree on the rock he'd used to raise himself.

Pain coursed through his body, but whether it came from being shot or from jarring his leg again he couldn't tell. Long moments passed in which he didn't care.

When he could next focus, he was lying sideways on the rock looking up at Arnold, who was considering him with an almost apologetic smile on his face. Dalton looked him over and saw the hand he'd clutched to his bloodied chest.

Then Arnold fell backwards and disappeared from view.

Dalton looked around for who had shot him. Quickly he saw that Tolbert had succeeded in his efforts to reach a gun. But his success hadn't cheered him, as he was hurrying along to kneel beside his brother.

Dalton looked beyond them to seek out the other hostages. Except now that he'd achieved his main aim, a weary feeling that started in his now thankfully numb leg spread through his body.

He rested his head on the hard rock, closed his eyes, and waited until Garrison arrived to pass judgment on him.

CHAPTER 16

'The major's not having us shot,' Tolbert said as he knelt beside Dalton's cot.

After all his exertions of the last few hours, Dalton could muster only a feeble nod. It took all his willpower to keep his eyes open, although he couldn't help but notice that Tolbert was wearing a military uniform again.

'And Mitchell?'

'I'm afraid he died.' Tolbert shrugged when Dalton started to murmur a commiseration. 'But then, that just means he got to do things his way again.'

'And the other townsfolk?'

'The rest of the hostages got away safely while the only survivor from Arnold's group was Deputy Rutherford, and he's in a bad way.'

Tolbert sighed, his downcast eyes suggesting he was trying to convince himself that this result compensated for Mitchell's death. But Dalton had no trouble in smiling now that he knew that the man who had started his troubles would receive justice.

Feeling more relaxed, he glanced down at his leg. Despite everything the splints were still in place and the limb appeared as straight as before. He felt no pain in the leg other than a dull ache. So he flexed his thigh and managed to raise his foot for a few inches and then lower it, also without discomfort.

'So why did Major Garrison change his mind about us?' Dalton asked.

'Because, Trooper Dalton,' Garrison said from the tent entrance, 'the cavalry needs more men like you and fewer men like Sergeant King.'

Dalton strained his neck to look past Tolbert at Garrison, who stood sternly to attention, considering the two men.

'Obliged you now see things that way,' Dalton said. He watched Garrison raise an eyebrow and this time Dalton had no difficulty in finishing his statement in the way the major wanted him to. 'Sir.'

Garrison gave a curt nod and came inside.

'The reason you were given the option to sign up, Trooper Dalton, was because it was claimed you had tried to kill Deputy Rutherford. If that isn't what happened, it'll be your choice as to whether you want to stay in the military.'

Dalton breathed a sigh of relief. Then, while sporting a pained look, he tried to convey that this time he was reporting honestly.

'Back in the law office last month Arnold King tried to punish Deputy Rutherford for disobeying him. I stepped in and saved his life. That was my only mistake. I don't want to compound that mistake by serving on, sir.'

Garrison considered him with a firm jaw. When Dalton responded with only an equally firm-jawed look, he flared his nostrils as a sign that, despite everything that had happened, he hadn't wanted Dalton to provide that reply.

'Then that is your choice.'

Garrison came to attention and saluted. Dalton raised himself on his cot to salute in return, as did Tolbert. Then at a brisk march the major left them.

'He didn't give you the same choice,' Dalton said guardedly while taking a long look at Tolbert's uniform.

'My circumstances were different as I really did shoot up my brother,' Tolbert said. He gave a thin smile. 'But despite that, he gave me the option. I decided to stay on.'

Dalton's mouth fell open with surprise.

'We didn't exactly enjoy our time in the military,' he said. 'We spent most of the time in the stockade, and the rest of the time we were either fighting for our lives or we were deserting.'

Tolbert laughed, acknowledging how unlikely this turn of events was, but then he stood and came to attention in a manner that was almost as crisp as

Garrison's had been.

'With Mitchell dead, I have no interest in staying on in Rocky Point.' Tolbert looked down at his uniform and batted dust from the sleeve. 'I need to find a purpose and, in a strange way, I reckon I might get one in Fort Lord.'

Dalton considered his friend. When Tolbert returned his gaze levelly, he gave him a brief and, he hoped, final salute.

'In that case, I wish you luck in your new life, Trooper North.'

Tolbert returned the salute. 'And I wish you luck in whatever you do next, Troop . . . Dalton.'